## Triathlon

The chanting, "Lono, Lono, Lono," followed Carl Lyons along the course, its rhythm penetrating his subconscious. The faces in the crowd of spectators went by him in a blur, and even the motions of pedaling were now automatic as his racing bike slipped through the humid Hawaiian air.

His mind drifted in and out of a trancelike state. In a lucid moment he sucked on a dry water bottle and then threw it away in disgust.

Lyons knew he had to be pushing himself like this for a reason. He combed his exhausted mind until he remembered—someone was in danger.

The Ironman pedaled harder.

**Mack Bolan's**

# ABLE TEAM

# THE IRON GOD

*Dick Stivers*

A GOLD EAGLE BOOK FROM

# W RLDWIDE

TORONTO • NEW YORK • LONDON • PARIS
AMSTERDAM • STOCKHOLM • HAMBURG
ATHENS • MILAN • TOKYO • SYDNEY

First edition October 1986

ISBN 0-373-61226-5

Special thanks and acknowledgment to
Tom Arnett for his contributions to this work.

# 1

Mauna Makanani drove the open Jeep behind the group of Russian bicyclists, wishing that at least two of the arrogant bastards would collide and fall under his vehicle's wheels.

Their head coach, Jaroslav Ocipovich, sat in the passenger seat; a large bullhorn rested across his lap. The back of the Jeep was packed with spare bicycle wheels, water bottles, an ice chest and about forty pounds of bananas. Two assistant coaches, driving small motorcycles, weaved in and out among the group of men on their fragile racing bikes.

The cyclists were averaging fifteen miles an hour, which Mauna knew was ridiculously slow for athletes who were about to take part in Hawaii's famous Ironman Triathlon. Mauna knew he could do as well, and he was only a canoeist, not someone who entered events that required the contestants to swim, cycle and run—all in one race. However, the Russians' head coach didn't seem concerned; he was more interested in the surrounding landscape than in the performance of his athletes.

Mauna was a native Hawaiian. He didn't see anything special about the landscape. Coarse grass had taken root wherever the lava outcrops permitted. On their left the deep blue of the ocean looked even darker than usual as strong winds whipped up a heavy sea. The foothills leading to the Kohala Mountains rolled away on their right. The grass was dun brown, an indication that it was, in fact, October.

The dry vegetation was bending under the force of the *mumuku*, but Mauna knew the cyclists couldn't use that as an excuse. It was only a breeze of twenty-five miles an hour, and it was usually windier than that during the actual race.

They had just passed the junction with Highway 19 and were nearing Puukohola Heiau, the Temple on the Hill of the Whale, when Ocipovich found what he was looking for. He bellowed something in Russian through the bullhorn, and all of the cyclists stopped. Mauna fought the urge to hit the closest Russians as he pulled the Jeep to a stop on the shoulder of the highway.

Following more directions from their coach, the cyclists gathered on a flat but rough piece of bare lava between the highway and the ruins of the temple. Mauna was uneasy. The war god's *heiau* was still holy to Hawaiians, and priests had forbidden foreigners to enter the area.

The guide wasn't sure that he believed in the old religion, but he was certainly not about to defy it. Far from dying out, it was gaining a new strength in the islands. The triathlon was even being held at the time of the full moon. There would be a special ritual at the Temple on the Hill of the Whale the night of the race.

Mauna climbed out of the Jeep and positioned himself between the Russians and the *heiau*. His left hand absently wrapped itself around the iron pendant that hung from his neck. His thumb massaged the small effigy of Lono, god of the harvest. The muscular Hawaiian's thoughts turned to the god, and he looked down at the carving. With typical native practicality, he told himself that he didn't have to be a true believer to wear the small pendant.

Mauna had never seen athletes train like this. It made no sense. First, the Russians lay on their stomachs in the ditches on either side of the road. The coach would consult a chart in his hand and shout something as he started his stopwatch.

Then the athletes would jump out of the ditch and group in the middle of the road. They would then run cross-country to the ocean before returning. Mauna was prepared to try to stop them, but decided their path would keep them south of the sacred ground. Still, he wished they wouldn't practice so close to the area.

Ocipovich stood north of the charging athletes, timing their lemminglike rush across the cracked lava flow to the sea. The bulky Russian with the sun-bleached hair was so intent on his stopwatch that he allowed the wind to pluck the paper from his hand. The *mumuku* carried it straight toward the sacred ground of Puukohola Heiau.

The coach dropped his bullhorn and was about to take after the paper when Mauna stopped him with a wave of his hand.

"Don't go! I'll get it."

Putting action to his words, Mauna took off after the piece of paper. It was a difficult chase. The wind was fast and the ground uneven. But the paper flattened against a gray lava stone of the ruins and stayed there as if held by an invisible hand.

Mauna reached for the paper. It was a chart that indicated a path from the road to the sea and a waiting boat. The Hawaiian moved to return it, but the invisible hand that had held the paper exerted pressure on his shoulder.

"The *mumuku* must be stronger than I thought," Mauna muttered.

But whether it was the wind, or his mind playing tricks, it was enough to cause him to pause and to look around. The athletes and the coaches had all stopped moving as if someone had called "freeze" in a game of frozen tag. Then they straightened and moved toward him, slowly, casually.

Too casually.

Mauna turned and fled toward the ocean. The chart fluttered in his hand. Not knowing what to do with it, he stuffed it down the front of his T-shirt. As he splashed into the surf, he heard the crack of a handgun. He was no fool; he wasted no time rubbernecking to see if he were the target. Instead he bounded through the shallow water as he headed toward the deeper safety of the sea.

Taking to the water had been instinctive, but it was his best chance. The men chasing him were all strong swimmers preparing for a triathlon that would begin with a grueling 2.4 mile ocean swim. But Mauna knew it was his only chance.

Mauna Makanani and his sister Nikko both worked as guides, although both had other ambitions. Nikko attended the University of Hawaii where she was studying anthropology. She was completely absorbed in the history of her native island. Her earnings were used to finance her studies.

Mauna's earnings allowed him to compete in canoe racing, the most popular sport on the islands. The five-foot-ten, 143-pound native with the long hair was all wiry muscle and determination. The sea was home, and swimming was second nature to Mauna. He had the added advantage of knowing both the water and the shoreline.

When the water reached his knees, Mauna plunged beneath a breaker, letting his chest skim the sand and volcanic rock bottom. The undertow pulled him eighty feet out to sea before he had to surface. It was a fifteen-foot swim straight up, but he controlled his wind and surfaced without problem.

The Russians who had treated him so coldly and contemptuously wouldn't have hired him if they hadn't wanted his Jeep for hauling supplies. Now they had the Jeep, and it seemed they also wanted him, he thought as he glanced back. They were standing hip-deep in the ocean scanning each onrushing wave, but they weren't looking far enough out to sea to spot him. Mauna swam straight out, fighting the fifteen-foot hills of water.

He heard a shout from behind him when he crested the first wave, then he started into the trough, out of their line of fire. The Russians were strong swimmers, but they were unfamiliar with the waters.

Mauna reached the point where the waves rolled almost parallel to the shore. He swam slowly as a wave lowered him into a trough. He took advantage of the next swell, turning with it and putting power into his strokes. He covered sixty feet of ocean before the crest dropped him.

The native swimmer was outdistancing the Russians who had finally taken to the water behind him, but he was also being paced from shore. He could not outdistance those on foot. He took the time to tear off his sneakers and jeans; they were easier to replace than his life. He continued the steady rhythm of relaxing while the ocean moved down under him and swimming hard when it raised him up. The swells suddenly changed direction, turning toward the island and carrying him closer to the men running along the broken shoreline.

When he reached the point where the waves were beginning to break, Mauna rolled onto his back and gauged each oncoming mountain of water. Finally he spotted what he wanted: a large wave that would break early. He rolled to his stomach and then extended his hands above his head and bodysurfed the wave, straight toward the beach at Waikoloa.

By the time Mauna reached the shallow water and stood up, the Russians were waiting for him on the crowded beach. Things would still be tricky, but he hoped for at least temporary refuge by moving in among the usual group of mid-morning bathers. The Russians had hidden their guns.

Mauna waded from the water. He was tired and was apprehensive about the confrontation he knew would come.

His left hand absently sought the comfort of the effigy around his neck as eight Hawaiians stormed over the sand carrying a canoe.

The group was known as the Kapu'ukus, or Sacred Fleas. They were the roughest gang on the island. When they weren't preparing for a canoe race, which was most of the time, they were out on their dirt bikes, terrifying anyone who crossed their path. Mauna knew them as he knew most of the canoe competitors. Usually he would exchange a greeting and then stay clear. In his present predicament they were a gift from the gods.

The leader of the group was a man named Ululani. His name meant "heavenly inspiration" in Hawaiian—a strange handle for the hulking youth, but the only one he had ever used. He was five foot eleven and weighed 230 pounds. His strength was such that it took three canoeists on one side of a canoe to balance Ululani's paddling on the other side. His paddle blade had twice the surface area of most paddles.

"Get me away from here," Mauna pleaded as he tried to catch his breath.

Ululani hadn't missed the Russians. "You got caught with some haole's daughter again," the gang leader accused between bellows of laughter.

"They've got guns," Mauna warned.

Ululani's eyes went flint hard, but he kept walking toward the shore. Members of the Kapu'ukus had already lowered their war canoe into the water.

"Come on," he told Mauna. "They won't start anything here."

The Russians watched helplessly as their prey was whisked back out to sea by eight strong paddlers.

JANE BRIGGS PAUSED as she adjusted the belt on the strapless green dress she had chosen for the day's outing. She glanced over at the man who was strapping an underarm rig over his bare chest.

"You're on vacation. We're here to have some fun. Why the hell are you going to cart a weapon around?" Jane demanded.

Rosario Blancanales, called Politician or Pol by the other members of Able Team, pivoted the mini-Uzi in the rig that had been designed to allow the small subgun to be fired without being drawn. If he had pulled the trigger, he would have shredded the potted palm in the corner of their hotel room.

Politician was five foot eleven. His graying hair made him look older than his forty-two years. He was often accused of mesmerizing people, of drawing them into the depths of his black eyes.

He was already wearing bleached chino pants that had pockets on both the front and sides of the thighs. The tan belt that held them up had two pouches attached. It matched his casual, ankle-high suede boots.

Hawaiian sunlight streamed through the floor-to-ceiling glass wall, highlighting the relief map of old wounds that decorated Politician's chest and back. Blancanales's hand stopped momentarily and then traced the scar of one wound.

"I'd feel naked without it," Pol told her.

He dropped a spare clip for the mini-Uzi into one belt pouch. Blancanales then walked over to the dresser and put a handkerchief, money, a small flashlight and a pocket-knife into his trouser pockets.

Jane clenched her teeth but didn't argue. She helped him into an off-white safari shirt. With the tail loose, the shirt concealed both the Uzi and the belt. Pol picked up his straight walking stick and headed for the door before he turned and looked at the woman who had quickly come to mean so much to him.

"And if there's any trouble, please do what I ask first and argue later."

"Why should there be trouble?" she demanded. "We're on vacation. We're on the island of Hawaii. Nothing ever happens here."

"You're probably right. But I stay alive by always hoping for the best and expecting the worst. I don't want to break the habit. It could be fatal."

"But we're on holiday," she repeated, her protest growing feeble, exasperated.

"Just humor me. Besides, we're keeping our guide waiting."

The short, well-built woman studied him with her green eyes. She knew she might as well concede defeat. He was so used to danger that he couldn't imagine living without it. What would life be like with him? She put any qualms she had about Blancanales to the back of her mind and smiled.

"Okay, I promise. But you have to tell me something."

"What?"

"Did you choose our nature-girl guide for her youth and good looks?"

"No. That's why I brought you along. Come here."

After a long, lingering kiss, they left their Kona hotel room. Jane's smile was still there, but it had relaxed.

**2**

The Place of Refuge was deserted when Rosario Blancanales, Jane Briggs and Nikko Makanani, their guide, arrived in the early afternoon. The national historic park was open, but it seemed that the tourists preferred the beaches and golf courses during the afternoon.

The thatched temple, sitting on the bed of lava rock and guarded by twelve large wooden carvings, looked as if it had been borrowed from another world. The palms in the background did little to anchor the site to the here and now.

"You brought us here before," Jane reminded their guide.

Nikko Makanani nodded. She was an attractive girl with long black hair that cascaded around her shoulders and down her back. She had a wide face and broad nose. Her dark eyes were set off by thick black brows. She wore a black T-shirt and faded jeans, and she carried a shoulder bag of coarse linen. Her feet were bare.

"I know," Nikko replied, "but it's not really out of our way, and I wanted to stop for a moment. I hope you don't mind."

"We don't mind," Blancanales said quickly. "I think we'll take a look inside the visitor's center for a few minutes. Why don't we meet back out here?"

Nikko nodded. She seemed relieved.

"What's all this about?" Jane demanded as soon as they were out of earshot.

"I was hoping you could tell me," Blancanales answered. "This place is still considered holy by the natives."

"So?"

"So I'm willing to bet the believers still come here when they're troubled."

"And you think our young guide is troubled?"

Pol nodded. "Don't you?"

Jane thought for a moment. "Now that you mention it, some of the sparkle's missing."

Jane and Pol strolled back to the temple area fifteen minutes later. Their guide seemed even uneasier.

"Like to tell us about it?" Pol asked gently.

She looked out to sea, not answering. Her hand played with a small iron figure that hung from a thong around her neck. The figure was similar to one of the large wooden effigies that surrounded them.

Suddenly the wind wrapped something around Blancanales ankle. He looked down at the yellow fabric, then bent and picked it up.

"It's *kapa*, a cloth made from mulberry bark," Nikko exclaimed. She reached out and touched the small piece of material. "It's very fine. It must be old. Maybe it's a sign."

"Do you believe in signs?" Jane asked. There was no mockery in her voice.

"Yes," Nikko admitted, but her voice had dropped to a whisper.

"Have you any idea what this might mean?" Jane persisted.

There was a moment's silence, broken only by the mournful sound of the wind and the relentless pounding of the surf.

"It's the royal color. Maybe Lono is welcoming a friend."

"Tell me about Lono," Pol said. "Maybe I'll recognize him."

Jane was shocked. "Don't make fun of her."

"I'm not." Pol gestured at the twelve carvings that towered above them. "Didn't you say these are the twelve faces of Lono?"

Nikko nodded and absentmindedly poked the scrap of yellow *kapa* into her shoulder bag.

"Then each person who knows Lono might see him slightly differently?"

"I hadn't thought of that. I suppose you're right. The spirits are treated strangely in Hawaii. No one really believes in them, yet none of us will risk offending them. I'm not the only *kana'aina* who comes here when troubled. Weird, isn't it?"

"Not particularly. None of us really understand the significance of our roots, but only a fool would deny their effect on his life."

The girl smiled. "You have unique ways of looking at things. It makes sense. Thank you."

"You're welcome. Is there anything we can do?"

"I don't think so. It's just that something's happened to my brother, and I have no idea what."

Pol waited, but no further information was offered. "Tell me about Lono," he said.

"Well, technically he's our god of the harvest, but actually he's a great deal more than that. He's the god who keeps this place of refuge. In the old days, if anyone insulted or outraged a king the penalty was death, but if he could reach this spot the priests would purify him. Then when he left, no one could touch him, not even the king. Defeated warriors who managed to reach this sanctuary escaped death, too.

"According to legend, every year Lono ran the circumferenceof this island, fighting anyone who wanted to take him on."

Blancanales laughed. "Sounds like Ironman."

Nikko was puzzled. "You know one of the athletes who's won the triathlon?"

"No, but the Ironman I know wouldn't be able to resist the triathlon. He thrives on physical competition. But he's really a warrior. I hope no one mentions this to Ironman. He's hard enough to live with now."

Nikko sighed. "I wish the *kapa* had wrapped around my ankle. I could use some assurance that my brother's okay. Any assurance."

"What happened to your brother?" Jane inserted the question so gently that Nikko didn't seem to notice.

"I really don't know that anything's happened to him, but I've been worried ever since the Russians came looking for him."

"Russians!" Blancanales's relaxed manner vanished.

"My brother also guides. Russia sent a whole group of athletes to compete in the Ironman Triathlon. The committee wasn't going to accept them until the State Department intervened. The Russians are here training.

"Anyway, they hired Mauna because he has a Jeep to haul around supplies for them. Mauna set off as usual this morning, but just before I left the house to pick you up four Russians arrived on the doorstep. They said they were looking for Mauna."

Nikko shook her head. Pol and Jane waited, not pushing her, but offering an attentive audience.

"I told them he'd already gone to meet them as usual, and they said he'd taken something and run away, leaving his Jeep behind. They said Mauna could have his Jeep back when he returned their property.

"I didn't know what to say. I simply shut the door on them. Mauna wouldn't steal. Even if he did, he wouldn't leave his Jeep behind."

Blancanales took Nikko by the elbow and began propelling her toward the parking lot.

"Let's see what . . ." he began, then interrupted himself to say, "I suppose those are the Russians."

"Yes. Not the four who came to the house, but those are the Soviet athletes. What are they doing here?"

It was a good question. Ten of them had climbed out of a yellow rental van and were spreading through the parking lot. The only other vehicles in the lot belonged to the staff and to Nikko. The Russians looked into all three before forming a line across the parking lot.

"I'd say they're about to sweep the place, probably looking for your brother," Blancanales answered.

He stepped to one side to see the operation more clearly. When he spoke again, the women had to strain to hear him.

"Jane, this is one of those times. Don't argue. Simply do. I'm sure these men are *spetsnaz*. You don't know me. Get in the car and get out of here. If you're followed, go straight to a police station. If I don't meet you at the hotel in an hour, call Stony Man."

Jane didn't answer or look at Politician. She looped an arm through Nikko's and steered her around a cluster of palms. The two women managed to make their stroll to Nikko's Pinto wagon look completely casual.

"What did he say?" Nikko asked.

A Russian stood close by. Jane could almost see his ears come to attention.

The woman sniffed and answered in a loud voice. "I won't repeat his words, but the proposition would be fun with someone we knew."

It took Nikko a moment to catch on. By that time they were at the car.

Jane stopped her questions by saying, "Just get us out of here before the Russians connect us to Rosario."

The two women jumped into the wagon and set off. Nikko swerved the small car around a bus that was pulling into the Place of Refuge parking lot.

"I hope he knows what he's doing," she said.

"So do I," Jane answered. "So do I."

Blancanales watched the two women leave the parking lot. He breathed a sigh of relief. He was severely handicapped as long as the enemy had merely to seize the women to neutralize him.

There was no question in Blancanales's mind—the Russian had recognized him as easily as he had placed the Russian. They had faced one another on a previous mission.

All the men searching the Place of Refuge were built like athletes. *Spetsnaz* alias athletes, Pol thought. The cream of the Glavnoye Razvedyvatelnoye Upravleniye, the GRU, the intelligence arm of the Soviet army. But why here?

Politician was now sure the Russians weren't in Hawaii simply to compete. He was equally sure that they weren't going to allow him to share his speculations with anyone else.

He glanced around casually, measuring his position and looking for anything that he could turn to his advantage.

The bus door opened, and a dozen elderly tourists climbed out. The men wore bright Hawaiian shirts, and the woman wore leis over their colorful muumuus. They listened intently to the guide's spiel.

The Russians continued to search the park grounds as if they were looking for someone. Blancanales decided that he wasn't the only haole who knew that Hawaiians still came to the Place of Refuge when troubled. They were undoubtedly searching for Nikko's brother. Politician knew that didn't mean they would forget about him.

Pol sauntered over to the bus driver who doubled as the group's guide. The man was waiting patiently while his passengers snapped their cameras and browsed through the information center.

"Would it be an insult to say someone resembled Lono?" Politician asked the driver.

The elderly Hawaiian was startled into honesty. "Maybe Lono would be insulted."

"Maybe he was. Anyhow, when I suggested that his twelve faces bore a striking resemblance to her side of the family, my wife took the car and left me here."

Blancanales handed the grinning driver a twenty-dollar bill. "I was hoping that I'd been here long enough to be absolved of my crime like the legend says. Do you think you could give me a lift to Kona?"

"Sure," the driver replied as the twenty vanished. "I couldn't refuse a lift to someone Lono's forgiven, could I?"

Politician joined the elderly tourists who were climbing back onto the bus. His reasoning told him he wasn't endangering them. The Russians wouldn't shoot him in front of witnesses, or risk a large-scale killing. It would blow their cover, and they hadn't completed their job yet. If they had, they wouldn't be wasting time worrying about whatever Nikko's brother had taken.

He settled back to relax during the ride. He knew he had to conserve his strength. He was relieved that the Russians hadn't sent their van after the two women, choosing instead to keep track of him. He was sure that they would follow him until he could be isolated from witnesses.

Ignoring the curious stares of the tourists, Politician held his straight cane between his legs and rested his hands on the brass knob that formed its head. He leaned his head back against the seat and forced himself to relax. He would need all the reserves he could muster if he wanted to stay alive.

**3**

Jaroslav Ocipovich was quietly, calmly furious. If one thing didn't go wrong, then something else did. He had been part of foiled plans before, and he was determined to let *nothing* spoil this job.

First, that damn native had made off with their chart. It plotted out the route of the kidnapping, and anyone who saw it would know it had nothing to do with the training preparations of a group of athletes. They had to find and eliminate the fool before he showed the chart to anyone.

Ocipovich knew that he had thoroughly planned the hunt for Mauna Makanani. When the native guide wasn't at home and wasn't hanging out with the other canoe racers, someone had thought of the Place of Refuge. Intelligence reports stated that natives still went there when troubled. More capitalistic superstition! However, his contempt didn't stop him from planning the search as if it were a full-scale military maneuver.

They had arrived at the site in two vehicles. The car had been left up the road, and the van had waited until those in the car had skirted the Place of Refuge to cut off another escape by sea. Ocipovich had acquired a great respect for Mauna's swimming abilities.

Ocipovich had been shocked when he had seen the American. The man hadn't even seemed nervous that there were eight of them and that he was alone. At least he had appeared to be alone, but Ocipovich had taken no chances.

There had been two women at the site. There was nothing to connect them with the American specialist, but they would be eliminated just in case.

The gray-haired warrior had been part of the team that had caused Ocipovitch and his comrades so much trouble during a previous mission. The team had been responsible for the black mark on Ocipovich's otherwise spotless record. The American was an opponent one could not afford to underestimate. He had to be eliminated immediately.

Under the guise of organizing the search, the light-haired *spetsnaz* leader had signaled for four men to follow the two women. The four had waited to make sure the native wasn't flushed and then had retreated back along the shoreline. They would take care of the women before any message could be passed on.

At least that phase of the operation had gone smoothly. If the gray-haired one was connected to the women, he could expect no help from that direction.

Ocipovich had been caught off guard when the man had calmly climbed on board a bus full of tourists. It was as if he had read the Russian's mind. There could be no witnesses. He was safe until he could be isolated.

The team leader signaled his men back into the van, and they took off after the bus. The American had done nothing more than buy himself a small amount of time. His cool would be quickly cured with hot lead. He would be dead long before the *spetsnaz* made their big play—the play that would permanently cripple American intelligence operations.

As the yellow van followed the tour bus along the two-lane blacktop toward Kona, Ocipovich organized his campaign. Two men would gather reinforcements and another vehicle. The rest would trail their prey until he could be isolated. Ocipovich had no desire for him to alert the rest of the awesome American special force that had caused the Russian's humiliation.

Still, the delays were dangerous. The entire *spetsnaz* force was supposed to be acclimatizing in preparation for the Ironman Triathlon. If they spent their time tailing people, questions would be asked. The business had to be finished quickly. It was true that many of the Russians would enjoy competing in the race, but if their mission was to proceed smoothly it had to be completed before the race began and the island became covered with reporters and television crews.

The bus stopped in front of the King Kamehameha Hotel to unload its passengers. Ocipovich left two men with the van and dispatched another to find reinforcements, while he and four others spread out and tailed the American warrior.

Their quarry didn't head into the six-story modern structure. Instead, he crossed the street and sauntered along Kailua Pier. The pier was heavily populated with the usual crowd of fishing enthusiasts. Long bamboo poles jutted from the pier; it would be hard to find an empty spot at this time of the day. Toward the end of the pier a trimaran named *Pu'ulima* was taking on passengers for a late afternoon and evening excursion.

Ocipovich and his men began to run when they saw the American's destination. They bowled over two tourists and knocked a fisherman into the sea. The skipper of the *Pu'ulima* was preparing to shove off. The gray-haired fighter spoke to him quietly. Money changed hands, and their prey stepped on board.

When the skipper saw even more passengers rushing his way, he patiently waited for them to catch up. He didn't approve of the way they pushed the crowd to one side, but a full complement of paying customers made the trip worthwhile. So he waited.

The skipper was a small man of Chinese origin. The hair that showed under his cap was sprinkled with gray, while the few strands of beard and mustache that attempted to sprout from his chin and upper lip were white. When he spoke, his voice was surprisingly full and the accent was pure American.

"Only four places left. Sorry. I'd lose my license if I took you all."

Ocipovich turned to his men. "You four take care of our problem. I'll handle things here." He spoke English because he didn't want to arouse anyone's suspicions by giving orders in Russian.

The leader paid sixty dollars a head for the four men who hopped onto the trimaran. He hoped his men would handle things discreetly.

The skipper leaped onto the deck as spryly as a man half his age and barked orders in Hawaiian. The crew slipped the painters and shoved the craft out from the pier. The wind had died to a steady southerly breeze. It ruffled the ti leaves tied for luck to the railing at the bow, and it billowed the three gaudy striped sails, moving the trimaran southward along the coast.

The American had moved a deck chair to the flat deck above the cabin. He sat with the boom swinging back and forth two feet over his head. Ocipovich watched from the pier as his four men each took a corner of the upper deck, waiting for things to quiet down.

Their leader turned away grinning. That was one more obstacle removed from his path. He wouldn't be caught like that again. One of his men was a talented artist. Tonight he would get him to complete sketches of the other members of the American team. By tomorrow every airport and tourist area on the island would be watched. If any of the others turned up, they would be eliminated before they knew they were even being watched.

The only problem remaining was the young native guide. Where in hell was he hiding? When he was out of the way, they could grab their man and be off the island before anyone knew that something had happened. Once he thought about it, Ocipovich was reassured. Even if the other American specialists were here, they couldn't do a damn thing to stop him.

"WE'RE BEING FOLLOWED," Nikko told Jane Briggs.

"You're sure it's not someone just going in the same direction?"

"Why do you think I'm driving around the block? I'm sure."

Jane craned her neck around and examined the car behind them. "I can't see that well, but I think they're all men. Let's go somewhere they can't follow."

"We can't spend our lives in the ladies' room."

"I wasn't thinking of living in a can. Let's pull into that shopping mall."

Nikko parked the car, and they sauntered toward the shopping area. There were no doors on the mall, but each business could be locked up when and if its owner decided to close.

The two women watched as the Russians stopped their car in a no parking zone. Three of the men jumped out. The driver stayed with the car.

Nikko and Jane strolled through the mall at a leisurely pace. If they knew they were being followed, they certainly did nothing to show it. Their first stop was at a florist shop.

"I must send flowers to a funeral home in Virginia. How quickly can you get them there?" Jane Briggs asked the proprietor.

"I'll telegraph your order immediately. They'll be delivered tomorrow."

"Tomorrow isn't soon enough."

"Ma'am, it's 3:30. That makes it 8:30 in the evening in Virginia. I'd like to help you..."

"Good. As long as you'd like to help, we'll manage." As she spoke, Jane handed the man a fifty-dollar bill.

"What's this for?"

"Your time and telephone expense. I'll pay for further services as I get them. You must have a list of florists. Look up Luray, Virginia, and read me the names."

The proprietor was too perplexed to argue. He placed the fifty-dollar bill on the cash register and pulled his directory of florists from under the counter.

"The Greenery, Phil's Flowers," he read.

When he paused, Jane said, "Go on."

"McSimmon's Wedding Bouquets, Norma's..."

"Stop! McSimmon's. Use that one."

"But, ma'am, you said it was a funeral."

"I did. Now telephone Luray. Offer the florist a hundred dollars to deliver tonight."

The man reached for the phone. "You are one determined lady. I'll do my best."

While the call was going through, Jane picked up a pen and scratch pad and wrote out the address and the message.

The call was answered on the second ring. When the request was relayed, the Virginian promised to tend to it himself. It would be done that evening. Then the Hawaiian florist read the name, address and message from the scratch pad.

"The card is very important," he said into the receiver. "It goes to Mrs. Carla Lyons, Stony Man Farm." The Hawaiian waited until the complete delivery address was read back to him, then he dictated the message. "Deepest sympathy on the probable demise of Rosario.... That's right, probable demise. Will do all I can to help. Love, Red. Got that?"

As he hung up the telephone, the Hawaiian florist looked at the small redheaded woman. She didn't look like the type who would let people call her "Red," but one could never judge.

He accepted the hundred dollars to send on to the Virginian, but returned Jane's fifty.

"I learned a lesson, little lady. The next time I have a customer who's in a panic and who's forgotten about time zones I'll know what to do. I figure I've already made enough profit."

The redhead flashed him the hottest smile he had seen in a long time. For once the Hawaiian was glad about his bald head. If he still had his hair, he was sure that her smile would have curled it.

He was still staring after the women when another fifty-dollar bill was shoved under his nose. The tall muscular man who stood on the other side of the counter wasn't smiling.

"What message my wife send?" the man demanded.

The proprietor sighed. She was a nice little lady, but not worth messing with this brute over. He picked up the scratch pad where the redhead had written the address and message. After a moment's hesitation, he handed it over.

"What it say?" the man demanded in a heavily accented voice.

The merchant recited the message quickly to hide the tremor in his voice. The man tore the top sheet off the pad and quickly left the shop.

THE RUSSIAN JOINED his two comrades, who were engaged in a heated conversation in front of a beauty parlor. Two of the men went off in opposite directions. One went to check for a back exit while the other went to tell their comrade to park the car and take his turn on watch. The third agent settled down on a bench that faced the shop.

The Russians knew that the women would have to come out before the beauty parlor closed.

**4**

The blue-and-white trimaran made good time sailing south along the coast. The streamlined hulls offered less resistance, yet provided wide deck areas to accommodate passengers. The forty-five-foot sailing vessel seemed spacious for the eleven passengers and four crew members.

Three passengers fished from the aft deck. Another three lounged on the front deck, sipping beer and talking about the evening scuba dive they were planning.

On the cabin roof, which doubled as the upper sun deck, Politician sat in a deck chair under the striped sails. He maintained a relaxed appearance, ignoring the four *spetsnaz* who crouched in the corners of the upper deck with their backs against the railing eyeing him like hungry vultures.

Pol's right hand rested lightly on the arm of the chair. He twirled his walking stick with his left hand.

He wondered if the highly trained Russians knew that the walking stick was merely a shortened *jo*. In the hands of a student of *jo-jitsu*, the inch-thick white oak stick was a deadlier weapon than a knife. The *jo* could be the deciding factor if Blancanales was forced to defend himself.

A short, smiling, barefoot crew member carrying a tray of alcoholic drinks moved from passenger to passenger. The four Russians each took a glass and pretended to sip. Politician smiled and asked for juice.

The crew member reappeared with a tall glass containing a mixture of pineapple juice and coconut milk. Pol raised his glass in a mock toast to the Russians and took a long drink. It was cool and refreshing. The *spetsnaz* stared at their alcoholic concoctions.

Ten minutes later Pol held up his empty glass and spoke to the Russians.

"I'm ready for another. Can I bring you fellows anything?"

They stared at him and scowled.

Before they had a chance to respond, Blancanales leaped to the raised part of the aft deck and made his way to the portable bar in the cabin. Two of the Russians hastily dumped their drinks overboard and followed.

The smiling crew member was restocking his bar with eight ounce bottles of mix. He set the small bottles on top of the bar as the passengers approached. Pol held up his empty glass and then placed it beside the mix.

"Another, please." He turned to look at the two *spetsnaz* with the empty glasses. "And I think these gentlemen expressed an interest in something stronger, perhaps with vodka."

The bewildered GRU killers found the glasses plucked from their hands. As the steward handed them fresh drinks, Politician deftly slid three unopened bottles of soda water from the top of the bar into the deep side pocket of his pants. He led the way back to the sun deck and settled once again in his chair below the boom. He sipped his juice and smiled. The Russians sipped their fresh drinks, and their scowls deepened.

Fifteen minutes later they made their move.

IN THE KONA SHOPPING CENTER some of the shops began to close. The women who worked in the beauty salon began to sweep and tidy the shop.

The Russian agents had regrouped in front of the shop, but in the ninety minutes that they had been waiting three more customers had entered the beauty parlor and five had left. No one had used the telephone, which they could see at the front of the salon.

Twice the Russians had used a pay phone to check in with Ocipovich. His orders were specific: unless the targets become suspicious, do not move until they are alone. If they try to communicate with someone, take the risk of killing them in public.

The last of the customers left, and there seemed to be only shopgirls remaining. But that was impossible. The Russians had watched carefully as each person left the shop. No one had left who resembled either of the women they had followed there. Two of the shopgirls had slipped out and done some shopping, but had returned with their parcels in time to help with the cleaning up.

A woman wearing a green shift had left the shop twenty minutes before closing time. Her dress had been similar to the one worn by the redhead, but it wasn't strapless and it didn't have a belt.

A *spetsnaz* had stopped the woman under the pretext of asking directions. The lady had been nervous and had had trouble understanding the Russian's heavily accented English. It didn't matter. The Hawaiian lady had been of Japanese ancestry, and therefore couldn't have been either of the two women they wanted.

The only other possibility had been an elderly lady wearing a muumuu. But she had been too old and too heavy.

The problem had exhausted the Russians' patience. One of the agents decided he couldn't wait any longer and strode into the shop just as the staff gathered at the door, ready to leave. Without a word of explanation, and ignoring the protests of the women, he stalked through the shop. No one was hiding there. He strode back and stood towering over the women.

"Woman with red hair and friend Hawaiian. Where they go?"

A small shopgirl, wearing too much makeup and an unbecoming Afro, spoke up. "I did her. She left forty minutes ago." Then the girl went back to chewing her wad of gum.

The Russian bent down and squinted into her brown face, trying to read her eyes through her tinted glasses.

"She did not leave here," he said firmly, carefully spacing his words.

"Sure she did. She sent Evy out for a muumuu and a sheet. She wrapped the sheet around her and then put on the muumuu. She had me make her hair white and put egg on her face to make her look wrinkled. She said it was a joke on her husband. You her husband?" The girl punctuated the question by blowing a bubble with the wad of pink gum.

"Not possible."

"Why? You missing some parts or something?"

Two of the other women giggled.

'What you say?"

"Why isn't it possible for you to have a wife? You look okay to me."

The GRU agent wanted to beat the American girl with his fists. He felt his ears grow warm. He looked around. A shopgirl with a wide nose and short black hair winked at him. He drew a deep breath and looked back at the girl who claimed to have transformed the redhead into an old woman.

"I mean I not believe she and old woman were same person."

The girl laughed in his face. "Hey, buster, I don't keep this job 'cause I'm beautiful. I keep it 'cause I know what I'm doing." She blew another bubble.

The Russian watched as the bubble burst. Some of what the girl had said was the truth. She certainly wasn't beautiful.

"And her friend?" he asked.

"What friend, buster?"

The girl who had winked at the agent spoke up. "She came in with a wahine with long hair. You didn't see her because she went straight out the back door."

"Both women go out back door?" the Russian asked.

The Hawaiian shook her head. "Just one. Just like we told you."

The Russian thought for a moment. It was possible that one or both of them had used the back door before his colleague had arrived to watch the rear. He decided that he believed their story. Why would they make up anything so complex? He examined their faces once more.

"If you're finished," an older woman said, "I have to lock up. My husband's waiting for me."

Whatever the explanation, the women were definitely not in the shop. They had been cool, not letting on they knew they were being followed until they were ready to give the men the slip. Without saying another word, the *spetsnaz* agent turned and stamped out, wondering what he was going to report to Ocipovich

The elderly beautician and the two girls who had talked to the Russian left together. After glancing around, the gum chewer disposed of her wad and took off the tinted glasses and handed them to the older woman.

"Thanks," Jane Briggs said

"You're welcome. You paid well for our help. But may I ask you a question?"

"Shoot."

"Wouldn't it have been easier just to use our phone to call the police?"

"I thought of that, but I'll bet that anyone who had used your phone would have been subjected to close scrutiny. I think they would have risked attacking us in broad daylight if they had thought we'd caught on. This way we didn't tip our hand until they'd lost us."

The woman smiled. "Sounds like you know what you're doing. Good luck. And your money wasn't wasted. You'll make a beautiful *kama'aina* when you take off the makeup. Be happy with it, because the dye will take a few weeks to wear off."

With that she left Jane Briggs and the short-haired native girl together.

"She's right," Nikko said. "You're going to look terrific. I wish I could say the same."

"Your hair will grow in. It's better than being really scalped."

"I know. Let's find the car and drive someplace where we can call the police."

Jane grabbed Nikko's arm. "Don't go near the car. They'll be watching it."

"You're right. Let's find a phone."

"I've already sent the only message necessary."

"You mean the flowers? I don't get that."

"We'll have help soon. I only hope it's soon enough. In the meantime, we need a place to stay tonight, and we have to find some way to hang around the airport tomorrow."

Nikko brightened. "Now that you're *kama'aina*, a native, I can take care of that. And I'm sure I have a friend whose clothes will fit you."

"I hope they get here in time," Jane muttered.

"YOU'LL KILL HIM with those things."

Lao Ti, five feet six inches of oriental dynamite, looked down at the heavy hunting knives in her hands as if she were seeing them for the first time. Then she looked Gadgets Schwarz in the eye and smiled.

"You mean these knives?"

She whirled and heaved one at Carl Lyons who was swigging from a bottle of Gatorade. The knife flipped once in the air and headed toward the warrior's chest, point first.

Lyons casually swung the bottle down, batting the knife to one side.

"Wait till I finish," he snapped. "I don't want to break the bottle. Hal will make me mop it up."

Gadgets collapsed into an easy chair in the Stony Man recreation room. He glanced from Lao's fragile-looking form to Lyons's towering hulk. With the shock of blond hair, gray pants and a bright red shirt, Lyons was difficult to overlook.

Lao wore jeans and a plaid shirt. Her short black hair was still damp from the shower. All three had just finished a grueling workout and had met back in the rec room after showering.

Gadgets had found Lao delivering a lecture in a dry, sharp voice while tossing knives at Ironman. He had been deflecting the knives with one hand while trying to finish his drink.

"Would you at least tell me why she's trying to kill you?" Gadgets demanded.

"Just an argument," Lyons answered.

Gadgets wore jeans, a denim shirt and hiking boots. His over-the-ears brown hair had been carefully blow-dried, which was why he had been the last person to reach the rec room after the workout.

"Couldn't you settle the argument more peacefully?" he asked. His voice betrayed the fact that he didn't expect a rational answer.

"It's the same thing we were discussing during the workout. I'm just proving that belief is more important than fact," Lao Ti told him.

She rarely bothered to explain, but Gadgets always found her few explanations worth hearing. He prompted her by remaining quiet and attentive, not his usual technique, but one he had learned was especially effective with Lao.

She tossed another knife with her left hand. Ironman automatically stepped to one side and let the weapon pierce the paneling as he casually finished his drink. Then he hurled the empty bottle at her.

Lao knocked the bottle to one side, allowing it to smash in a corner of the room. The action failed to interrupt her short lecture.

"If you ask an ordinary man if he can bat aside a knife thrown at him, what will he tell you?"

"If he's got more brains than Ironman, he'll say he can't do it."

"Why would he say that?"

Gadgets rolled his eyes. "I don't know too many people who enjoy having knives plunged into their chests. Without all that martial arts jazz, it would be hamburger time."

"Wrong. Training doesn't give the ability. It gives the belief you can do it."

"Shit!"

"At over twelve feet, most people would have sufficient reaction time. If they don't dodge the knife, it's because of one of three things: insufficient concentration, indecision or non-belief in themselves. Training gets rid of the indecision and gives the person belief that he can do it. It doesn't make him a superman. Has training changed your reaction time or your decision-making ability?"

Gadgets sat quietly, not saying a thing. Lao and Lyons didn't interrupt. They knew it was Gadgets's way of assimilating Lao's message. Lyons winked at Lao. She returned the slightest trace of a smile, which for her was the equivalent of a grin. Their knife-throwing act had triggered an acceptance in Schwarz. He was absorbing a concept that he had rejected with fast talk and patter when they had been on the practice floor.

Suddenly Lao flipped a knife at Gadgets. It wasn't the lightning throw she had been using on Ironman, but the Bowie knife would cut skin if it finished its flight. Gadgets batted the knife to one side so violently that it flew across the room and clattered against a wall twenty feet away.

"Belief," Lao said in a gentle voice.

Gadgets stared at his hand as if it were an alien object.

"Yeah. Belief," he muttered.

"Now that we've settled that, how about a swim before turning in?" Lyons asked.

"Hey, we've just finished a two-hour workout and I've just showered. Don't you remember?" Gadgets complained.

"Just a two-mile race for the fun of it."

Gadgets groaned. "I'd have a better chance racing a shark. My belief refuses to stretch that far."

He was saved from further argument by the arrival of Hal Brognola, the Stony Man assignments officer. Brognola carried a wicker basket of white lilies and pale pink gladioli. A wide satin bow with long streamers was tied to the basket's arched handle. Gadgets took one look and burst into laughter.

"Are you mourning or celebrating?" he asked Brognola.

The federal agent ignored him and turned to Lyons. "These just came for Mrs. Carla Lyons."

"What's the gag?" Lyons rumbled.

"Wish it was a gag. Read the card."

Lyons picked up the card and glanced at it. Then he handed it to Lao. She read it aloud.

"Deepest sympathy on the probable demise of Rosario. Will do all I can to help. Love, Red." She looked up. "Is this a joke?"

Lyons shooks his head. "We've got to get to Hawaii."

"Explain," Brognola snapped.

"The Communists must have Blancanales.'

"You think Jane Briggs sent this?"

"Who else?"

"It doesn't say anything about Communists," Brognola objected.

"You weren't here when Ironman called Jane 'Red,'" Gadgets told him. "I thought she was going to get a ladder so she could bust him in the nose. She won't let anyone call her 'Red.' She can't stand its connection to communism."

"Why didn't she phone?"

"She's being watched. Why else would she say she'll do all she can. Move," Ironman snapped.

Hal Brognola made for the door, calling over his shoulder, "I'll arrange for an air force jet."

Able Team scrambled to the armory to assemble their weapons.

"We need our own plane," Gadgets complained. "We're going to be too damn late."

## 5

Rosario Blancanales knew the Russians would make their move the moment they thought no one was watching. Fifteen minutes after Pol returned to the sun deck with the purloined soda water in his pocket, the *spetsnaz* found their opportunity. They moved in on Politician from the four corners of the upper deck.

Pol waited until the last second, then lunged from his chair. He went into a deep squat, thrusting his *jo* like a fencer's sword.

The tip of the white oak stick rammed into a jackal's gut, paralyzing the brachial plexus and canceling the man's ability to breathe. Unable to utter a sound, the Russian stumbled backward and toppled over the low side rail. The body turned one complete flip and slid quietly into the ocean, feet first.

Blancanales didn't stop to watch one enemy die; he had three more to fend off. The thrust of the *jo* was turned into a powerful backhand sweep as Pol spun himself into the empty corner of the upper deck. The three remaining *spetsnaz* jumped back quickly to avoid the whirring stick.

Others on the small craft were occupied with fishing, drinking and just relaxing. The crew was beginning to prepare the evening meal. No one had noticed the Russian sliding quietly into the sea. No one noticed the quiet, desperate battle on the top deck. The Russian commandos certainly didn't want to attract attention. Pol made no call for help; he didn't want any innocents killed.

The gray-haired fighter crouched in the corner, letting the boom swing over his head. The *spetsnaz* decided it would be risky to approach the deadly stick without a chance to spread themselves out. Again they sat down on the deck, alert, waiting for Blancanales to relax.

Crouched in the corner of the sun deck, constantly alert for the slightest movement from the enemy, Pol realized he had to leave the boat. There was too much chance that someone would see the fight. The Russian goons would then decide to eliminate the witnesses. On a boat this size the highly trained killers could do it.

The tense quadrangle held its shape until the *Pu'ulima* sailed into a small bay. The water was calm and clear. A small coral reef closed off much of the entrance to the natural harbor. Blancanales suspected the area was deserted largely because it would be difficult to navigate past the reef to reach the cove.

Pol took advantage of the distraction of the crew dropping anchor to leap to the rear deck and confront the captain. He kept his voice loud, wanting to be certain that the Russians knew he wasn't passing a message to the Hawaiian skipper.

The Able Team commando thrust two fifty-dollar bills into the captain's hand.

"I'm leaving your relaxing voyage at this point. Here's fifty dollars for the use of your dinghy and another fifty dollars for whichever member of your crew rows me ashore and returns the dinghy to the *Pu'ulima*."

The small skipper eyed the two fifty-dollar bills suspiciously.

"What's wrong?" David Waihee demanded

Politician laid on his most disarming smile.

"Not a thing. I like your ship, I like your hospitality, and I'm sure the food will be excellent, but I must be put ashore immediately."

"Why?"

"Two fifty-dollar bills. I feel I'm free to come and go as I see fit. I'd prefer not to swim ashore, but I will if I must."

"Your funeral," Waihee said, waving the money, "but this tip gets divided among all the crew."

"You're a wise man, Captain."

Waihee grunted, then turned to a crew member.

The man leaped to the top deck and tossed the inflated boat into the water. He sprang down to the aft deck and into the life raft before it could drift away. Blancanales gave the captain a nod of thanks and leaped into the dinghy.

The *spetsnaz* moved quickly in an attempt to board the inflated boat.

Two of them yelled at the captain. "Stop that boat. Order it to return."

"I didn't pay for their company," Politician called to Waihee.

By then the captain understood that the hundred dollars had come tightly tied to a large bundle of trouble. He barked another order in Hawaiian to the oarsman, who suddenly started to row the awkward craft as if his life depended on it. Waihee smiled at the shouting Russians.

"You go next trip," he told them. "Where's your friend?"

The Russians' grasp of English was minimal, but they knew there would be trouble over their comrade's disappearance. They exchanged quick glances and then dived into the warm ocean water and started crawling for shore.

The *spetsnaz* were trained swimmers, but hampered by clothing they were no match for the Hawaiian rowing the dinghy. Politician stepped onto the rocky beach a full thirty seconds before the arrival of the first pursuer.

The Hawaiian oarsman rowed furiously along the shore, making a wide detour of the three swimmers. As Politician turned his attention inland, he thought wryly that it hadn't taken the captain and his crew long to recognize that the Russians were dangerous.

Pol found the going slow over an old lava flow that had made it as far as the beach. Every footstep had to be carefully placed. The purplish-brown rock was filled with ankle-turning and foot-snagging fissures. He knew that the terrain wouldn't help his chances of survival.

Blancanales also knew that the enemy would be armed. They were obviously in Hawaii to do more than compete in a race. The absence of witnesses would leave the *spetsnaz* free to take up target practice on the isolated lava field. The Stony Man warrior didn't relish being their pigeon.

He almost stumbled into a large opening in the ground. A lava tube! Nikko had told Politican and Jane that the tubes were formed when the surface lava cooled while the lava beneath continued to flow. It resulted in hollow tubes and pockets.

He looked back. The three agents had spread out and were closing the gap. Each had an automatic in his hand. Pol hadn't shown his weapon yet. He knew that any element of surprise could make the difference.

However, the lava tube did present an opportunity. He looked for another that would supply better cover and altered course for what looked like the perfect spot.

His change of course helped the Russian athletes. They were within twenty feet of him and grinning like hyenas before Politician finally reached the tube. It varied from four to seven feet in diameter, went into the side of a flow and then turned slightly.

Without hesitation, Blancanales entered the cave. Before he had even made it around the bend, one of the pursuers was in the tube after him. The cave ended four feet after the bend.

The pursuer slowed while his eyes adjusted to the dim interior. Politician couldn't afford to take such luxury. He whirled, pivoted the mini-Uzi in its holster and fired a short burst at the figure at the mouth of the tube. The Russian grunted and staggered out and away from the opening.

Excited voices and screams of agony filtered into the cave. Blancanales, unwilling to be trapped, crawled slowly back toward the opening. He tried to raise his head enough to see what was happening, only to have two 7.62 mm slugs come close to parting his hair. The slugs whined around the cave like angry hornets trapped in a bottle.

As Pol crawled backward to reach the safer area around the bend of the tube, an automatic barked once, silencing the screams of the wounded Russian. His comrades didn't want the noise to attract attention.

Blancanales huddled and waited. There was no use trying to make a break for it. The cave had put Pol out of reach of their bullets, but he was effectively bottled.

And then the Able Team warrior remembered the three small bottles of soda water that he had pocketed aboard the *Pu'ulima*.

Blancanales was fully aware that he was buying only seconds and minutes. It was improbable that he would stay alive long enough to be rescued. But the Able Team warrior also knew that long odds were the worst possible reason for giving up.

A soft voice, not even winded from the chase, whispered into his cave, "Old one, are you awake?"

The question was followed by laughter.

"Sometime you sleep. Then we get you."

There was another angry chuckle, then nothing more.

Pol sat with his back against the wall of the cave and waited. They would get him, but not without a fight.

6

Princess Sherrie Lilivokalani had returned to her native Hawaii in the only way royalty should—she had flown first class. Her subjects were at the airport to meet her.

There could be no doubt that the blood of ancient kings was rich in her veins. Six feet tall, she came nowhere near King Kamehameha's lengendary height of seven foot five, but she stood well above the five members of the Hawaiian Historical Society who escorted her. Hawaii was now part of the great republic, and her royal domains were the historical and cultural roots of a noble race.

At one time yellow feather leis were worn solely by royalty. Now they had been adopted by the members of the historical society as a symbolic tie with their heritage. One of the five society members presented Princess Sherrie with a yellow feather lei. It was a showy gesture and purely symbolic. Certainly the lei stood out from the mass-produced ones that were being handed to tourists at Keahole Airport.

Sherrie Lilivokalani wasn't a beautiful woman, but she had presence and an air that demanded and received instant respect. At fifty-two her shoulder-length hair was still a rich black. She wore a white wide-brimmed hat to protect her features from the sun. Her white linen suit and her high-necked blouse were obviously expensive. The princess's wide mouth had a habit of quirking at the corners, and the wrinkles around her eyes were proof that she possessed a good sense of humor.

The princess and her retinue strolled slowly through the crowded but open terminal. Hawaii's climate made a regular terminal building unnecessary. To prevent sunstroke, shopkeepers and ticket agents were provided with small thatched huts Walkways were lined with flowers and lush greenery.

She paused to observe the disorder of deplaning rituals. People milled around watching the progress of their baggage as it was unloaded. Time was spent talking to friends, waving to acquaintances and examining the leis presented by the handsome young men and women employed by various travel companies and souvenir photographers.

The scene was broken by the scream of another jet coming in for a landing. It was unusual for one plane to follow another so soon; everyone in the terminal turned to look. A mat black executive jet touched down so lightly that shock absorbers seemed unnecessary. It killed speed toward the end of the field, then turned and taxied toward the terminal.

Typical of haoles, so anxious to enjoy themselves that they push others out of the way, Lilivokalani thought to herself. She sometimes wondered if the laws of the old kings weren't best. Execute barbarians when they disrupt things. Keep them from changing native islanders in ways they shouldn't change.

The logo on the side of the black craft spelled out Acme Exterminators.

"It's a strange world," one of the historical society members remarked. "People who kill insects are able to travel in that style?"

Whoever the executives of Acme Exterminators were, they continued to show their impatience. The door of the Sabreliner opened, and three people jumped out without waiting for steps to be wheeled into place. They neither looked nor moved like the executives the princess did business with.

Sherrie Lilivokalani noticed that the man in the lead was probably two or three inches taller than she was. Blond hair blazed in the sunlight; at this distance it seemed as if his head bore a crown of flames. He wore brown pants and a Hawaiian sport shirt. Despite the casual cut of the shirt, it appeared unnecessarily loose. The heavy boots that completed the outfit looked out of place with the rest of his clothing. His stride moved him through the mob at a pace faster than many could run. He constantly surveyed the crowd, and Princess Lilivokalani knew he was looking for someone. There was the distinct impression that those frigid blue eyes missed few details.

He was followed by a very thin but muscular oriental woman who wore her hair short and sculpted to her head. The princess thought the woman was a mixture of races. The woman wore jeans, tennis shoes and a loose blue work shirt. Although she was much shorter than the blond man, her smooth stride kept her directly behind him.

The final member of the trio looked from side to side as if he expected to be jumped at any moment. He sported styled brown hair and a full mustache and wore cream pants with a matching safari jacket. His leather shoes had crepe soles.

All three carried small gym bags. The strained shape of the handles told Lilivokalani that the bags were heavy. The strange trio had so caught and held her fascinated attention that she had stopped walking and stood staring as they approached.

Two of the women employed by travel companies to greet passengers hastened to intercept the trio. The taller of the two women whispered to the other one loudly enough for the princess to overhear, "He really could be Lono."

What a ridiculous thing to say! Lilivokalani thought.

The shorter of the two placed herself squarely in the path of the onrushing leader. "Aloha," she said as she held up a lei.

Princess Lilivokalani took a second look at the young woman. Something was wrong. The girl had a mainland accent.

The tall man came to a stop, but he didn't seem to see or hear the woman with the garland. Something else in the crowd had caught his attention.

Before Lilivokalani could turn to see what it was, the man reached over with one hand and lifted the regal yellow lei from around her neck. He flicked it over his own head.

The suddenness of his strange action left the princess speechless, but explanations flashed through her mind at top speed. Her first thought was that in the days of the old kings he would have been killed for such an action. But then the old kings had killed commoners for much smaller breaches of etiquette than lifting a lei. His shadow had fallen on her. That alone would have been sufficient to stage an execution. Only a god's shadow could fall on a royal personage. Her thoughts returned to the present when the strange man raised his gym bag into the air.

MAJOR JAROSLAV OCIPOVICH FOUND himself performing an uncomfortable duty that he usually assigned to one of the *spetsnaz* under his command. What with searching for the missing Hawaiian guide, looking for the two women who had given his men the slip and watching the airstrips and other tourist spots for the rest of the American team, his thirty troops were spread very thinly.

So the *spetsnaz* leader found himself on airport watch; it was a boring and unrewarding job.

He was worried about the men he had put on the sailboat to take care of the gray-haired opponent. They should have reported in by midnight, hours ago. He had been on the move, but he expected that someone would have told him if they were back. He would investigate as soon as his relief came.

Ocipovich had watched the 747 spill its payload of tourists. None had remotely resembled the team of specialists that had caused him so much trouble in the past.

He looked at the crowd around him with thinly masked contempt. Americans were a decadent lot; it was no wonder they were losing the public relations battle with the Soviet Union. The brat beside him was a prime example.

The kid had red hair, freckles and the disposition of a wolverine. He carried a scuba diver's spear gun that would have cost a skilled worker three weeks' pay in the Soviet Union. The boy also carried a wicked-looking spear for the weapon. His mother had told him repeatedly not to load the gun. Four times, when her back was turned, the boy had fitted the spear to the gun and had tried to stretch the two bands of surgical elastic over the firing trigger.

Ocipovich dropped his contemplation of the homicidal ten-year-old to concentrate on three people who seemed to be attracting everyone's attention in the open terminal. The GRU major's blood pressure hit an all-time high when he recognized the group. It was the remainder of the dreaded American team! The Russian's trained eye and his experience told him that their three gym bags were loaded with weapons. How had they caught on so quickly?

He looked at the face of the tall, fair one. The blue eyes seemed to find him in the crowd. Ocipovich could not walk away from the challenge. He snatched the spear gun from the junior warmonger beside him and snapped the two firing bands into place.

The spear gun was raised with the smooth, practiced motion of someone skilled at firing weapons all of his life. He pulled back on the trigger.

CARL LYONS EXPLODED into action when the spear hissed from the Russian's gun. The Able Team warrior blocked the surrounding noise and movements from his thoughts as he concentrated solely on the pointed missile. Whether it was Lao Ti's philosophy or his own experience was now irrelevant. With one deft movement, Lyons deflected the spear from the air with his gym bag. He dropped the bag and took off after the attacker.

"Watch her," he yelled over his shoulder at his teammates.

A female voice behind him squealed, "It really *is* Lono!"

Her shout immobilized every native Hawaiian within earshot. It had the chain effect of stopping curious tourists. Lyons shot through the frozen mass of onlookers.

Gadgets picked up Lyons's bag and stepped up to the woman. "Stay close to me," he ordered.

"What's happening?" a member of the historical society asked, her voice verging on hysteria.

Princess Lilivokalani glanced curiously at the spear she had picked up from the ground and said, "Calm down, Grace. We'll go with this gentleman and find out what it's all about."

Gadgets led them to a place between two thatched huts that turned out to be a newsstand and a flight-insurance booth. He kept his eyes peeled for further danger. Lao followed, watching the other direction. They stayed there, quiet and alert, until Lyons came striding back.

"Lost him. A busload of tourists walked between us."

"Why are you keeping us here?" a member of the princess's entourage demanded.

"Thought you might be in danger. You can go."

The members of the historical society began a hasty retreat. When they realized their president wasn't following, they turned to find that she was still with the rude, blond haole. Still clutching the fishing spear, she looked Lyons straight in the eye.

"The lei?" the princess asked. "You thought it made me the target?"

"It was very unusual. I was wrong."

"How do you know that? Wait...don't answer. You can tell me at the luau. Shall we say tonight at seven-thirty?"

"I'm afraid that won't be possible," Lyons replied.

"I'll be disgraced if you refuse to come."

"You must go!" one of the girls distributing the leis exclaimed. She was determined to follow the blond "god."

"He'll be too busy," the shorter flower girl said.

The words caused Lyons to look at her more closely.

"Jane?"

"The same."

All three of the people who had arrived on the black jet burst into laughter.

"That crazy suntan!" Gadgets exclaimed. "Even your hair's fried black."

Jane Briggs joined in the laughter. "I can dye my hair back to its natural color, but it'll take two weeks for the color to work out of my skin."

The tall girl with Jane still had not torn her eyes away from Lyons. She disengaged her left arm from the leis and pointed toward the distinguished Hawaiian woman in the white suit and hat.

"Princess Lilivokalani. You will need her help."

Lyons cocked an eyebrow at Jane.

"Ironman, this is Nikko Makanani. We think her brother is involved in this, and we were both tailed by the Russians."

Lyons stared at the native girl. "You don't think we could make better use of our time than by feeding our faces?"

"You must," Nikko answered simply.

Lyons turned back to Lilivokalani. "We accept."

She took Lyons's hand with hers. "I'm so glad. What hotel? I'll send a car."

"King Kam," Jane said.

"Wonderful. By the way, whom shall my driver ask for?"

"Smith—" Lyons began.

He was interrupted by an icy voice that demanded, "Lyons, what the hell are you doing here?"

Lyons was the only member of the group who didn't turn to face the speaker. He didn't need to look around to recognize the man behind the booming Bostonian accent.

"Princess—" Lyons began, only to be cut off a second time.

"I asked what you're doing here?"

Lilivokalani also ignored the interruption. "Please call me Sherrie. Hawaii doesn't really have a royal family anymore."

"I'm Carl Lyons. The idiot with the loud voice is Ernest Cowley IV, CIA briefing officer. Call him E-4."

"That's classified information!" the man with the Boston accent exploded.

Only then did Lyons turn to face the Company man. He was taller than Lyons, but of a slighter build. His light brown hair was carefully parted, and his skin deeply tanned from hours spent in the sun practicing for triathlons.

Lyons had been told that Cowley spent his mornings training and his afternoons at his desk. Looking at the lean athlete's body, Lyons believed it. Cowley wore a white golf shirt, conservative brown shorts and proper knee socks. His brown loafers gleamed. Lyons had the strong feeling that wherever Cowley went a part of Boston went with him.

Ironman's eyes and his voice were at their coldest. "You shouted my name out, so I took for granted we were engaged in a publicity campaign."

Cowley's skin turned a shade darker. Ironman couldn't tell whether the flush was caused by embarrassment or anger.

When Sherrie Lilivokalani spoke, her voice sparkled with amusement. "I already know Ernest. His father and I went to Harvard together. How is your training going, Ernest?"

"Ahh, fine. Excuse me, Sherrie. I have to talk to this man."

"Be sure that your shadow doesn't fall on him, Ernest. It might be fatal." She turned to Lyons. "I'll send my car for you and your party... Mr. Smith. I'm looking forward to it." With that Princess Lilivokalani left the airport, escorted by her entourage of amateur historians.

Lyons spoke before Cowley could open his mouth. "What are you training for? Moron first class?"

Cowley looked around uncomfortably. He was followed by four men, who were sweating in their suit jackets. They were obviously armed bodyguards. E-4 was a demanding boss. His escorts were trying not to smile at Lyons's wisecrack.

"So I spoke too hastily," Cowley admitted, "but that was no reason to jeopardize my safety. Now, I want a straight answer. What are you doing here?"

Lyons stared at the taller man without answering. The Able Team warrior was tempted to use the federal agent as a punching bag. The man had blocked their access to needed information once before. Although he was high in the CIA chain of command, Lyons wasn't sure whether he was a friend or an enemy. As either he was dangerous. It was conceivable that he had something to do with Blancanales's disappearance. Lyons would put nothing past the CIA snob.

Gadgets spoke as if he had been reading Ironman's mind. "It's almost time for the Ironman Triathlon. Your girlfriend asked Cowley how his training was coming."

"His girlfriend?" Cowley seemed amused but quickly dropped the subject. "Lyons are you going to answer my question or not?"

"Not," Lyons turned away. Gadgets could be right. The man was probably only here to train for the race. But why trust him?

When Able Team was out of earshot, Cowley snarled at one of his bodyguards. "I want to know what they're up to. Tell Williams to handle it."

**7**

The Able Team group took a taxi directly from the airport to the hotel. Booking rooms on such short notice required a lot of persuasion—the folding paper kind. Then, assembled in Jane Briggs's room, they were briefed by Jane and the young Hawaiian woman.

The whole damn thing boiled down to six questions. Where was Blancanales? What were the Russians really after? What had Nikko's brother stumbled across that made him a target? Was Mauna Makanani still alive? And, finally, was that bastard Cowley a piece of the puzzle?

Carl Lyons didn't trust the CIA officer; gut instinct made him send Lao Ti to locate the pompous blowfish. Lyons hoped that she might be able to spot a connection.

The rest of the group ended up at the pier in front of the hotel thanks to a tip from a local who made it his business to know everything that was going on in Kona. After questioning several people about the *Pu'ulima*, the group finally located the boat and its captain.

Preoccupied with his hunt for Blancanales, Lyons launched into the conversation without wasting any time to introduce himself. "What can you tell me about a gray-haired man who took your cruise yesterday?"

The skipper didn't even look up. "Talk to HPD. They've already wasted enough of my time."

Captain David Waihee continued to paint the railing of the *Pu'ulima* until he found himself lifted by the shoulders of his windbreaker.

"About my friend?"

Without saying a word, the captain whistled. Five seconds later two men appeared on deck. One held a Colt 1911, the other an M-16. The skipper waited until Lyons was covered before speaking.

"Put me down."

Lyons obliged. The small captain looked up, eyes sparking with fury.

"You look more like the men who followed your so-called friend onto my trimaran. You want answers, you talk to the police."

Lyons decided he had better try to repair the harm caused by his impatience just as Nikko placed her hand on his sleeve. He turned and looked down into the young Hawaiian's warm brown eyes.

"Don't worry. Captain David is a friend of the princess. She will help."

Waihee turned his back, muttering loudly enough for everyone to hear. "What does Sherrie have to do with this?" Then he leaped onto the stern of his trimaran and continued his painting, totally ignoring the group on the pier.

The two crew members still had their weapons trained on the group. Lyons shrugged and strode back along the pier. After a moment's hesitation, the rest of Able Team followed. It was a frustrating retreat.

The members of Able Team had always acted on the assumption that another member would be there to pick up the slack in a sticky situation. Blancanales was the one who would have managed to gain the skipper's cooperation. But Pol was missing, and they needed his skills to find him.

"Where are we going?" Jane Briggs asked.

"Sherrie's."

"But we're not expected until this evening."

"We need her help now."

"We can go back for my car," Nikko decided. "I don't care if the Russians find us now."

"Brave words," Jane scoffed, but she immediately hailed a taxi that took the group to the shopping mall and the Pinto they had abandoned twenty-four hours earlier. It didn't seem as if anyone was watching the car.

The short drive south along Highway 11 to the island's famous coffee-growing area was completed in gloomy silence. Each member of the group contemplated the fate of Blancanales and the young Hawaiian guide. Just east of Honalo, a battered mailbox shared a rotting post with two orchids in full magenta bloom. The faded name on the side of the box read Lilivokalani.

The crushed stone driveway ended in a parking lot that was concealed from the house by a hedge of Japanese holly. A short flower-lined walk led them to the manicured yard, complete with a large pool, and beyond that, to the house itself.

The two-story house was shaped like an *H*. The middle section featured lanais on both the ground and top floor. The deep porch areas were enclosed by Moorish arches topped by straight, narrow columns. Giant smokethorn trees stood guard around the house, leaving visible only the occasional patch of white stucco or window that opened to catch the breeze.

The princess was in the lower lanai straightening the lounge chairs and wicker furniture. She strode across the lawn to meet them.

"What a pleasant surprise," she said as she greeted the group. "I didn't expect to see you again so soon."

"We need your help," Lyons said as she took his hand.

"I'll be glad to do what I can, but you're not going to talk business without something cool to drink. What will you have?"

She led them to the cool shade of the lanai and motioned for them to sit down. Without being summoned, a stout, dignified native in a muumuu took their orders and quickly returned with the drinks.

The princess waited for her guests to lose some of their tension before asking, "And what may I do?"

"The man we're here to trace took a cruise on the *Pu'ulima* and didn't return. I was too abrupt with the captain. He referred us to the Hawaiian Police Department."

"And that isn't sufficient," Lilivokalani finished for Lyons.

He shook his head. "It involves Russians who claim to be on the island for the triathlon. We've crossed swords with at least one of them before. It's best if we handle things our way."

Sherrie sipped her Scotch, studying him over the rim of the wide glass.

"The *Pu'ulima* was at the Kailua pier just now?"

Lyons nodded.

She consulted an expensive looking wristwatch. "David doesn't usually have a cruise this afternoon. He schedules evening cruises twice a week. I'll phone him. Excuse me."

The princess strode into the house, leaving her guests to finish their drinks. Lyons took a long pull on his beer, then wiped the foam from his lip with the back of his wrist.

"I'd feel better if I knew why she's so helpful," Gadgets muttered.

"He deflected the spear and prevented her from being harmed. She has an obligation to throw a luau and do whatever she can to help. It's the least she can do for Lono," Nikko answered. Her tone said she was stating the obvious.

"Who's Lono?" Gadgets asked.

"A local deity," Jane Briggs answered.

"Run that by me again," Lyons said.

Jane didn't even try. She glanced at Nikko, passing the buck to her. For the first time the Hawaiian guide showed signs of embarrassment.

"I explained all this to Mr. Blancanales. He seemed to understand. Lono is our god of the harvest, but he's much more than that. According to our legends, he celebrates the harvest by running around the island and taking on anyone who dares to challenge him at *lua*."

"At what?" Jane interrupted.

"The Hawaiian martial art," Lyons answered. He kept his attention focused on Nikko Makanani.

"There are other traditions and rituals. When Lono arrives at a village, one of the local warriors throws a spear at him. Lono catches the spear and presents it to the local chief or family leader. In our rituals, Lono is played by someone who's been trained to catch the spear. The person who receives the spear is under obligation to hold a luau in Lono's honor and to do whatever is necessary to please the god. Mr. Lyons didn't catch the spear, but he did protect her."

Jane frowned. It was obvious that the talk of Polynesian gods disturbed the Hawaiian girl.

"The princess seems like a sophisticated lady. Surely she doesn't believe in this Lono business? She asked Ironman his name. She doesn't call him Lono."

Nikko opened her mouth to say something more, but was forestalled when Lilivokalani interrupted from the doorway.

"I'll field that one, Nikky."

Her presence automatically made her the center of attention. The princess glided onto the lanai, taking time to survey her guests' drinks. Finding that none needed to be replenished, she settled on a chaise longue. Although she spok· tc everyone on the open porch, she kept her eyes fixed or Lyons.

'First, David Waihee the skipper of the *Pu'ulima*, is on his way over. He'll answer your questions as a favor to me Please don't antagonize him further.

"As for my beliefs, or the beliefs of my fellow islanders for that matter, you must understand that Hawaiians are a superstitious people."

She paused to sip her Scotch. The others were so held by the force of her personality and the smooth educated lilt of her voice that they forgot their own drinks.

She set down her glass and continued, "Carl is very much a man in my eyes. That doesn't mean he cannot also represent much more. When he deflected the spear so that it would land at my feet, he fitted himself to one of our myths. I could easily have ignored it and walked away.

"I think like the Hawaiian I am. Carl doesn't have to be either a god *or* a man. He doesn't have to be either a warrior *or* a pest exterminator. He can be as many things as his nature allows.

"Native Hawaiians enjoy the best of the past and present because they make no attempt to separate them. Our old religion is enjoying a revival, yet those who attend it still think of themselves as Christian. There's going to be an ancient religious celebration after the race. None of those who attend will really regard themselves as superstitious, just practical.

"I'll throw the luau. Everyone will have a good time. No one will care whether the reason for the feast is legitimate. And we'll all make new friends."

She paused, took a deep breath, then added, "That's what this princess believes. And please just call me Sherrie."

The lecture was over, and a silence fell on the group. They sipped their drinks quietly until a vehicle turned into the driveway. From the lanai they had a brief glimpse of an open red Jeep before the vehicle disappeared behind the hedge that screened off the parking area.

David Waihee walked slowly across the yard. He nodded to the group, but waited until he was seated and holding a glass of Scotch before speaking.

"So you haoles really can get Sherrie to jump when you snap your fingers."

If Lilivokalani was disconcerted by his words, she didn't show it. She merely smiled and sipped her drink. She had given Able Team a chance to mend fences; she wasn't going to try to do it for them.

"We still want to find our friend," Lyons said. "We don't want to involve the police. It would require too many explanations."

Waihee sipped his Scotch and said nothing. His hazel eyes never left Ironman's face.

Lyons nodded at Jane Briggs. "She sent for us. We flew from the mainland to help. Apparently our friend boarded your evening cruise yesterday. So did four other men— Russians. None of them returned. The Russians have probably killed him, but we need to know for sure. They wouldn't risk killing him unless they were after something important."

Waihee sighed, finished his drink and stood up.

"Don't have time for fairy stories. I'll tell you just one thing. If your friend does show up alive, HPD wants to talk to him about the disappearance of one of my passengers."

Lyons was frustrated but managed to conceal it. "You'd better explain that," the Ironman said as he sat forward in his seat.

David Waihee looked Lyons straight in the eye. "I'll lay it out for you short and sweet. Your friend boarded just before we cast off. Five others came rushing up—all men, all young, all fit, like you. I had room for only four. The leader paid me and put his four men on. He stayed behind."

Lyons interrupted to describe the Russian who had been at the airport.

"Yeah. That's the guy who paid the fares.

"Anyway, I take the *Pu'ulima* down near Ka Lae, the southern point of the island. I know a little bay there that no one goes to much. There's a small coral reef for those who want to try night diving. It's always calm. Good place to serve the grub.

"When we get there, your gray-haired friend pays me a hundred bucks to put him ashore. I try to talk him out of it, but he just smiles and asks would I rather he swim. It's his business. He paid, so I had one of the hands prepare to row him to the beach in the life raft.

"As they were shoving off, three of the big guys who don't speak much English come up. I got the general idea that where your friend goes, they go, too. They dived overboard and swam after the dinghy.

"I don't see them again. I don't see the fourth Russian again either. He must have been tossed overboard when we were under sail. That's why I reported it to HPD."

Waihee stopped talking and drained his glass. "Now you got the whole story."

"Can you take us there?" Lyons asked.

"No point. Whatever happened, happened."

"You're now my friend," Lyons answered. "You want me to take that attitude if you disappear?"

"Hell, no! We'll take cars. It'll mean a walk at the other end, but it'll still be faster."

"We'll all go." Sherrie Lilivokalani decided. "We'll take my car and David's Jeep."

"Thanks, but . . ." Lyons began.

''If you want my help, we'll do it Sherrie's way,'' Waihee interrupted.

Lyons decided he wasn't going to waste any more time arguing. He headed for the parking area.

## 8

MAJOR JAROSLAV OCIPOVICH sat in his hotel room grinning at Friedrich Vorovski. The little political commissar was part of the support staff for the operation. Ocipovich had made him equipment keeper, a position he felt fitted the talents of a political appointee. The Russian major knew he should not offend the bald-headed gnome. The man would report such an action directly to the party.

"Granted," Ocipovich said, "the operation started badly. We could foresee neither the guide's stupid action nor the interference of the American team."

Vorovski snorted into his drink, a repulsive concoction that the bar called a grasshopper. The political member of the unit felt it was his duty to personally research the stories of Western decadence.

"Badly is an understatement, comrade. You tell me that at least two of your men are dead and the man who killed them is still alive.

"First, you let a mere native run away from the feared *spetsnaz*. Swim away, actually. Some athletes! Then, while you are looking for him, you show your face to someone who has discredited you in the past.

"Your army-trained espionage specialists were unable to keep track of two mere women. They lost both before they could be eliminated quietly. I suppose we should be thankful that you knew these things should be done quietly.

"Then you, personally, bungled an easy execution at the airport and drew attention to yourself. I would say that this whole operation has been plagued by your inability to command."

"I think you are being harsh, Vorovski. I was assigned men who have an insufficient grasp of the language. And I will admit that unexpected events caught me 'flat-footed' as the Americans say. But it is results that count, and we are about to produce them."

Vorovski looked up from his drink and cocked a bushy eyebrow.

"What have you done, prayed for a miracle?"

"I will leave the praying to you, comrade. We have merely carried out our mission."

"And how many men has this glorious victory cost?"

"We have lost only the two who were careless with the gray-haired devil. We knew that he was part of a team of particularly ruthless and violent fighters. The men were warned."

Ocipovich hurried on before the political appointee could interrupt. "That leaves ten of the twelve men posing as athletes. We still have the six of us who double as coaches and six who act as bicycle mechanics and equipment managers."

"Seven," Vorovski interrupted.

"Of course. Seven, including yourself. We also have five GRU agents who have gone undercover as Russian journalists. So you see, we still have ample manpower."

Vorovski hated losing a point. "We were talking results, not your wasteful use of manpower."

Ocipovich grinned He enjoyed making points. "First, the gray-haired demon has been cornered and will soon be eliminated. One of the surviving pair telephoned from Naalehu, near the southern tip of the island. I have dispatched additional men to the area. They will help eliminate the enemy and should return shortly.

"Second, the rest of the American specialists were spotted at Kailua Pier. One of the missing women, the native, was with them. They are being followed and will be eliminated later.

"Our pigeon is training for the triathlon at Puopelu Ranch, a resort just north of Parker Ranch, near the Kohala mountains. He is well guarded, but it will be easy to abduct him when he is being driven to the place where he does his training swims. We are even prepared to make the snatch in the water. There is nothing the American specialists can do to prevent it.

"Our athletes will compete and go home. No one will even suspect we are involved."

"So all this optimism is based on the probable death of one enemy and on knowing where to find the rest of his team?" Vorovski's voice was scornful.

"There is one other thing," the *spetsnaz* leader said. His voice was so innocent that the political commissar looked at him suspiciously.

"And that is?"

"The rest of the support staff have located the native who took our attack chart. At this moment the net is closing in on him. Within the hour he will be in our hands. He will be taken at this point."

Ocipovich's finger pointed to a map of Hawaii's west coast. Vorovski leaned forward and glanced at the map.

"You mean this place they call the Place of Refuge?"

## 9

"You know we're being followed?" Waihee asked Carl Lyons.

Lyons looked back. Lilivokalani's Mercedes, driven by the princess herself, was immediately behind them. Gadgets rode in the front. Jane Briggs and Nikko sat in the back. A quarter of a mile behind the Mercedes, a small red sports car paced them.

"CIA," Lyons grunted.

"They're not supposed to be operating here now that we're a state. You sure?"

"Who else would be so obvious?"

"What are we going to do about them?"

"Stop some place. I'll chat with them."

The skipper frowned. "How do I know you just want to talk? I don't really know who the hell you are."

Lyons pulled the big Python from a pancake holster in the small of his back. He flipped the gun and handed it butt first to the driver.

"You control the situation."

Waihee took the gun with his right hand. Steadying the steering wheel with his wrists, he expertly snapped out the cylinder, ejected a cartridge and weighed it in his hand. He replaced the bullet, returned the cylinder and then transferred the heavy revolver to his left hand before sliding it into a pocket on the door of the Jeep.

"Okay. You get your chance to talk. Wave to Sherrie to keep going. We should sandwich the idiot between us."

Lyons took out his communicator and passed the message through Gadgets.

They were doing a steady sixty along the highway. Waihee slowed and swerved the open vehicle up a bank of loose green rock out of sight of the road. He immediately killed the engine.

The Mercedes, followed by the sports car, raced past their concealed position.

Waihee started his Jeep and drove back onto the road to pursue the small M.G. When the driver of the sports car spotted the tail, he downshifted and pushed the gas pedal to the floor. The small red car disappeared around the next bend.

"We still have someone behind us," Waihee commented as he glanced in the rearview mirror.

"Damn!" Lyons exclaimed when he saw the yellow van. "By the time we get this mess cleared up, we may never find Pol's trail."

ROSARIO BLANCANALES HAD THOUGHT the night would never end. The Able Team warrior knew that one of the two surviving Russian hardmen had gone for reinforcements. Things were looking increasingly hopeless, but Politician wasted no thought on the outcome of the battle. A warrior knows that he is already dead; his life is measured in bonus heartbeats.

Blancanales had been alive once. In those days he had been a Green Beret in Nam—a medic and a hell-raiser. That was when he had discovered that he possessed a gift for languages. Within a few months he had become fluent in Vietnamese and French and had even managed to make himself understood in the dialects of the mountain peoples.

Along with the ability to communicate with the Vietnamese, he gained a genuine empathy for their plight. Vietnam had been torn by wars, internal and external, for as long as the people could remember. Despite that they remained a stubborn and unbroken people. Politician began spending all his spare time in the villages, using his simple medic skills and strong back to help the people endure. It was there that he met Sergeant Mercy.

To the enemy, and to many American GI's who didn't understand him, Sergeant Mack Bolan was the Executioner. His specialty was deep penetration behind enemy lines, and his targets were usually high-ranking Communist officers or corrupt politicians. The young specialist was the most feared man in the area

Most Vietnamese were victims, not aggressors. To them Mack Bolan was Sergeant Mercy. He was the GI who helped them put their villages back together after a raid. He cared for their sick and did what he could for the orphans created by the horrible civil war

Then Rosario Blancanales found himself recalled to headquarters for reassignment. There he met a young practical joker who had been yanked from another company. The troublemaker was Hermann Schwarz, better known as Gadgets.

Both men jumped at the chance of joining Bolan's deep-penetration unit. Their bond with the Executioner was hammered out in the jungles of Nam deep behind enemy lines, where every step was taken with caution and every breath savored as if it might be the last.

Fighting behind the North Vietnamese lines was not the kind of work approved of by insurance companies. Politician spent most of his time on pacification programs and penetrating enemy territory. He gave himself up for dead every time they left on one of those kill missions. Only later did he discover that it was his attitude that kept him alive.

Acknowledging that he was already dead made him a formidable warrior.

Veterans of other wars had returned to heroes' welcomes. The press had made much of an America ashamed to stand by her friends in Asia. The conscripts who managed to return from the Vietnamese hellgrounds found themselves greeted at best with embarrassed silence, at worst with outright hostility. Those specialists who did find jobs found themselves doing menial, repetitive tasks for which they were no longer suited.

Blancanales became a hospital orderly, aging from the inside out, fading because of the undemanding nature of his work. When the call came that Mack Bolan was forming a squad to help fight the mob, Blancanales walked out of the veterans' hospital without even collecting his pay.

He had suddenly realized that he had become only half alive. Bolan's cause was hopeless, but it was worthwhile. Once again he became a warrior. The commitment would never again wear off.

The Death Squad broke the powerful Mafia empire in California, but the huge battle also broke the Death Squad. Only Bolan, Schwarz and Blancanales survived.

Now, crouched in the small cave in the dark of the Hawaiian night, Politician relived those epic battles. And he relived the missions he had been a part of as a member of Able Team, a group of dedicated warriors who now fought urban terrorism on the home front.

Mack Bolan had teamed Rosario Blancanales and Gadgets Schwarz with Carl Lyons, an ex-cop with no military experience. Able Team clicked. It had the right balance of skills and temperaments. Lyons had been born dead. He zeroed in on what mattered and paid absolutely no attention to anything else. This made him an articulate genius of strategy whose ability was well hidden behind the disposition of a crazed maniac. Only Politician and Gadgets had the special ability to accept and flow with the loose, intuitive leadership of Ironman.

Lately Lao Ti had proven her ability to fit into the special relationship enjoyed by Able Team. A strange, taciturn comrade-in-arms, she proved to be as economical with words as Lyons. Strangely she and Lyons seemed to understand each other, although Blancanales wasn't sure if Ironman would ever fully accept Lao as a member of the team.

Blancanales had made one bottle of soda water last the night. He had known that the cave would become an oven in the day and that he would need the water to replenish lost moisture. Ultimately it wouldn't matter. Dead men don't need moisture. And if that was to be his fate, the Able Team warrior was determined to make his death count for as many enemy as possible.

The number of voices outside the tube had increased. Pol counted at least four. He met two demands to surrender with absolute silence. He knew they weren't there to take prisoners.

Someone tried to fire into the cave in an effort to hit him with ricochets, but the angle was wrong and a patch of pumicelike rock at the end of the tunnel absorbed the bullets instead of bouncing them.

After that barrage, they tried to talk to him. Blancanales neither answered nor returned fire. He saved his energy and his bullets. He would wait until they came to him. The Able Team warrior opened another bottle of soda water and sipped it sparingly. The temperature in the cave rose, but not as much as he had expected. Still, the cave was by no means comfortable.

The voices spoke Russian. Politician had acquired a smattering of Russian, but the voices were too soft and distorted for him to follow the conversation. They seemed to be arguing.

Pol heard the Russian words for "dead" and "asleep." His quiet was beginning to pay off. The light in the cave dimmed. Someone had entered, cautiously, noiselessly. Politician pointed his mini-Uzi at the bend and waited.

A Makarov was thrust around the corner. Pol was already as low as he could comfortably sit. He did nothing. A bullet made no difference to a dead man, but missing a chance at an enemy did.

The report, confined by the walls of the tube, caused Blancanales's ears to ring. The bullet broke off fragments of rock, which stung the side of his neck. Pol ignored the pain, concentrating entirely on the visible weapon.

It pointed toward the roof, apparently forgotten as the gunman listened for a reaction. Blancanales remained silent, but he brought the small Uzi up to bear on the corner.

There was a small shuffle and then the Russian poked his head around the corner at exactly the point where the Stony Man warrior had trained his weapon. A three-round burst removed a corner of the man's skull.

Excited voices rumbled back and forth in fast Russian. There was a flurry of activity outside the cave. Blancanales waited quietly. He could hear them throwing things at the mouth of the tube. He rolled onto his stomach and peered around the corner with his head flat to the floor. But there was no one watching for him. They were too busy throwing branches and bushes into the mouth of the cave.

The Russians were going to smoke him out.

It took Ironman a split second to make his decision. "We'll take out the red car. We won't mess with the van unless it gives us trouble."

Waihee gunned his Jeep and reached into the door's side pocket at the same time. He passed the Python back to Lyons.

Surprised, Lyons accepted it.

"Why?" he asked.

"I figure trouble's coming down on us fast. I'd rather that cannon was in hands that can make good use of it."

Ahead, Lilivokalani suddenly jammed on the brakes and slewed the Mercedes across the two-lane highway. The driver of the red M.G. had to do some fancy braking to keep from smashing into the sedan. By the time he had the sports car stopped, Waihee had brought his Jeep to within two feet of the driver's door.

Ironman vaulted out of the Jeep and closed in on the driver's side of the small car. Gadgets jumped out of the Mercedes and held his Beretta 93-R on the passenger side of the M.G., steadying his hand on the roof of the German-made car.

"Well, well," Ironman said. "Perhaps you can explain yourself, Mr. Williams."

Stew Williams, wearing his usual three-piece suit, scrambled out of the small car. Able Team had worked with the amiable CIA operative before.

"Just doing my job," Williams began.

"Tell us later," Lyons interrupted.

He gestured for Williams to get into the Jeep.

Crouching to reach into the low sports car, Lyons knocked the gearshift to neutral, then straightened and walked around to the front. He put a combat boot on the shiny hood and shoved. The small car ended up in the ditch.

Williams opened his mouth to say something, thought better of it, turned and climbed into the Jeep beside Waihee.

Lyons checked the highway. The yellow rental van had stopped well back. Whoever it was, they were simply keeping tabs on them. Signaling to the princess to continue, Lyons vaulted into the uncomfortable seat behind Williams. Waihee took off again without instructions.

"Give," Lyons said into the CIA operative's ear.

Williams was as tall as Lyons and had blond hair and blue eyes, but no one would ever confuse the two. Williams had the round face and innocent expression of a child. People instinctively liked and trusted him. Lyons's face was well formed. He was large and handsome, yet something of his cold nature showed in his frosty eyes. Lyons was the material from which tales of men of iron had been fashioned.

"Nothing to give. I was told to keep tabs on you. I did what I was told." Williams's voice was carefully neutral.

"And they suggested you use a bright red sports car to do it?"

"E-4 didn't specify."

Lyons snorted. "What's up?"

"I honestly don't know. E-4 issues orders, not explanations."

Lyons lapsed into silence. He knew Williams wasn't as tame as he seemed. It didn't matter how he tried to keep tabs on Able Team; he would have been spotted sooner or later. But Lyons wasn't overlooking Williams's clever way of accomplishing a difficult assignment.

The two vehicles pulled off the road half an hour later. They parked beside a rental sedan. There was no sign of the car's driver.

"We walk from here," Waihee told his passengers.

They were half a mile from the cars when a burst of autofire rattled on their left. Lyons and Gadgets broke into a run.

Lyons's Python was held tightly in his left fist, and Gadgets had his Beretta 93-R out. As they sprinted toward an old lava flow, their nostrils detected smoke. They smashed through a fringe of shrubbery and climbed the flow.

Ahead of them, four men lay in prone firing positions, covering a bonfire with automatic handguns. Only one vulture heard the two warriors burst from the sidelines. He jerked his Makarov around to track on the intruders.

The Makarov never targeted. Before the swing was complete, Lyons's revolver barked twice. The first .45 Magnum slug helped the *spetsnaz* killer to roll over. The second smashed into the center of his chest as he tried to sit up, spilling buckets of blood through a fist-sized exit hole.

The roar of the Colt commanded attention. All three remaining Russian killers swung their attention and their guns toward the intruders. At the same time the bonfire erupted into a geyser of flames as a human figure exploded from its depths.

The Russian goon squad wasn't sure who to shoot first. They hesitated only a fraction of a second. A fatal fraction of a second.

Gadgets's MAC-10 sent one *spetsnaz* a final message. The would-be assassin looked down in puzzlement at his bullet-riddled body. He died before he realized what had happened to him.

Lyons's Python swung smoothly to the next target. A single shot blasted out the back of a Communist skull.

The Russian specialist closest to the fire jumped when a burning ember fell on him. Then he twitched and writhed as Blancanales pumped three short bursts from his mini-Uzi into him.

Politician looked around and then used his gun barrel to flick a couple of sparks from his slacks.

"You two sure know how to keep a guy waiting."

MAUNA MAKANANI HAD KNOWN that the Russians would watch his apartment and so he had spent the night with a friend. When he had returned home the next day, he had found his Jeep parked outside the building. The keys had been left in the ignition.

The young Hawaiian guide didn't question his good luck. He simply decided to spend the next few days with a girlfriend at Keanapaakai. The small village was located just west of Mauna Loa, the island's most active volcano. "Mauna," Hawaiian for mountain, was a popular male name on the island. Everyone secretly hoped that their son would grow like a mountain and be as large in stature as the Hawaiians of past centuries.

Several times on the trip south, Mauna spotted a green Ford in the rearview mirror. He thought nothing of it until he turned off the highway onto the rough road leading to Keanapaakai. When the Ford also chose that road, Mauna decided he was being followed. He didn't know how he had been spotted, but he wasn't about to stop and ask. He stepped on the gas, suddenly wanting to be surrounded by other people.

Mauna Makanani didn't reach Keanapaakai. Five miles from the town, a rented pickup blocked the road. The men waiting for him were two of the athletes who he had worked for.

They had chosen their spot well. The ditches on either side of the road were too steep to take without rolling. Mauna stopped but knew he didn't have time to turn the vehicle around before the green car blocked the road from behind. Safety posts lined either side of the road.

Mauna took the only other option open to him. He leaped from his Jeep and ran for the coffee fields below. Neither group of pursuers was close enough to use handguns, but they were athletes. Four of them took off on foot after Mauna. This time there was no ocean to escape to. Mauna sensed that his survival depended on keeping ahead of these highly trained Russians.

Under the hot noon sun, Mauna played hide-and-seek with four grim-faced killers. He decided to head for the sea about nine miles to the west. It meant leaving the cover of the coffee trees, but the instinct was strong, and he yielded to it.

Several times he thought he had lost them only to find they had spread out and were methodically pursuing him. When he looked down, he discovered that he was actually helping the men. His borrowed jogging shoes had a distinctive tread pattern. He was leaving unique footprints as he raced over the cultivated soil.

He had no choice but to increase his pace. His throat was parched. His small image of Lono bounced against his chest, urging him forward. The four large men followed him at an easy pace, wolves content to let the deer wear itself out.

The Russians had been on alert since midnight, waiting for the beeper they had planted on Mauna's Jeep to indicate that the vehicle was being moved. Once Mauna had picked up his wheels, they had simply called in the reserves and had boxed him in until they were sure of stopping him in a deserted area. He had cooperated beautifully. But not everything went in the *spetsnaz*'s favor.

Mauna had rested well, eaten lightly and taken in a great deal of fluids. He was in good shape for a cross-country jaunt. Running wasn't his sport, but he did jog for stamina. In the still heat of the plantation and over the broken fields, the native managed to preserve his slight lead. The wolves seemed unworried.

The deadly race kept up for two hours. The roar of the ocean grew louder. Mauna crossed Highway 11 too exhausted to do more than stumble on. He considered flagging down a car but rejected the idea. If the car didn't stop, the pause would be fatal.

He staggered across the highway, causing a large car to lock its breaks and skid to an emergency stop on the blacktop. He paid no attention but willed his body to keep going. The four wolves were now less than twenty feet away. They seemed to have found their second wind and were moving in for the kill.

This hadn't been the paced exertion of a sporting event; it had been the all-out drain of reserves of a primitive escape-or-perish chase. The sea was just ahead, but Mauna knew he no longer had the strength to commit himself to it. He glanced around wildly, searching for any promise of shelter he could find.

And then he remembered. Just to the north was Pu'uhonua o Honaunau, the Place of Refuge.

In the oppressive heat of the afternoon, there were no tourists wandering around the site. The parking lot was nearly empty. Even the staff had retreated to the visitor center to escape the heat. The place was deserted, primitive, menacing.

Mauna made his legs carry him across the rough lava bed toward his destination.

"Lono!" he shouted from a parched throat. "Lono!"

**11**

Nikko and Jane Briggs rode in the Jeep with the skipper on the return trip to Princess Lilivokalani's home. Williams was assigned the front seat of the Mercedes where Able Team could keep an eye on him. Lyons and Gadgets flanked Politician in the back seat, demanding to be brought up to date immediately.

Blancanales quickly and concisely gave them all the information he had. Williams frankly turned around and took it all in. Lyons didn't like sharing the information with the CIA, but it was safer than letting Williams out of his sight.

Politician finished his story, and the three warriors began speculating on possible Russian targets. They didn't get far; their attention was diverted when Sherrie stood on the brakes.

The car skidded but held a straight line, coming to a halt with its bumper just short of a crazed young Hawaiian who staggered across the road, seemingly oblivious to their presence. He was quickly followed by four athletic-looking men.

"The *spetsnaz*!" Blancanales shouted.

The skipper's Jeep stopped inches short of the Mercedes's rear bumper.

As Lyons baled out, he heard Nikko shouting, "Mauna! Mauna!" But the runner didn't seem to hear her. Lyons could tell that the young Hawaiian was suffering from an advanced state of exhaustion where the body is driven only by its will to survive. He had been down that road several times himself. Without further thought, he pulled out his Colt Python and sprinted after the Russians.

Gadgets jumped out of the sedan and then immediately dived back in.

"They're heading for those buildings. Get there first," he told Lilivokalanı.

She pushed the accelerator to the floor and took off for the entrance to the park. Waihee kept his Jeep right behind them

"The Place of Refuge," Politician told Gadgets. "Strange he should head there."

The moment Sherrie squealed to a stop in the parking lot, Gadgets, Politician and Williams scrambled from the car and raced to the far end of the historic site. Waihee and the three women followed as far as the edge of the parking lot, where they could see the action.

Lyons was well rested compared to the hot and weary Russians. His long legs propelled him over the open terrain. A *spetsnaz* wolf looked around and didn't like what he saw.

There was menace in that easy, ground-eating stride and the silent way the chase had been joined. The hunter decided he didn't enjoy being the hunted. He stopped and brought his Makarov to bear on the striding blond figure bearing down on him.

The young Hawaiian and the other three hawks disappeared around a high stone wall. The Hawaiian started to shout something in a cracked, desperate voice.

But the large pursuing figure with the hard blue eyes never broke stride. The big revolver in his fist acquired a target and roared its displeasure.

The *spetsnaz* suddenly heard the Hawaiian clearly. He was calling "Lono, Lono." The Russian never heard the

Colt Python. A 230-grain lead eraser wiped those concerns from his mind.

Lyons rounded the end of the stone wall to find one killer zeroing in on Mauna, leaving the other two to cover outside interference. One leveled his automatic at the group racing across the parking lot while the other stepped behind the wall to eliminate whoever had been following them.

Carl Lyons didn't intend to be eliminated. He came past the end of the wall in a low dive and roll as 9 mm corpsemakers snapped the air above his head. He tucked, did half a roll on the hard rock surface and came out of it in a prone position. The huge revolver calmly swung to point at the killer against the wall.

The Russian kept the trigger of his automatic depressed and directed his line of fire toward the American. He fought the climb of the Makarov and zeroed in on Lyons's forehead. He then met with a minor technical difficulty.

The Makarov is an automatic, not a machine pistol. It cycles its eight-round magazine at the rate of one shot every two seconds. Between the time one bullet ate air over Lyons's head and the next bullet was discharged, Lyons calmly placed a .45 slug into the gunman's eye, ruining his aim and his entire day.

The two surviving *spetsnaz* decided Lyons had them outnumbered. They forgot the young Hawaiian and their weapons and scrambled over the stone wall like a couple of frightened squirrels. Lyons let them go; it was time to reload.

After he had used a speed loader to recharge the revolver, he eased around the wall. His caution was unnecessary. He was just in time to see the two fugitives pile into the yellow van that had been following them. The vehicle sped away.

Lyons took an exhausted Mauna Makanani by the arm and led him to the parking lot and his frantic sister's em-

brace  Then ironman turned to Williams and handed him
the Python

"Return it when you're through with it," he told the
startled CIA operative. "You'll find us through Princess
Lilivokalani "

"Through with it? What am I going to do with it?"

"The police will want to see it when you explain why you
had to take out these Russians," Lyons answered as he slid
into the Mercedes.

The sedan and the Jeep sped away, leaving a bewildered
CIA operative looking up the highway toward the sound of
approaching sirens

"I CAN'T MAKE anything out of it, either," Gadgets said,
passing the Russian chart to Ironman. Mauna Makanani
had given them the piece of paper that had caused all of the
trouble

"They're going to hit a car or truck, but where? Why?"
Lyons asked.

They were sitting on Sherrie's lower lanai, once again enjoying her hospitality. The veranda area was spacious, but
the group seemed to fill it. The servant was nowhere in sight,
but a cart of bottles and mixes had been wheeled out when
they had arrived.

Blancanales was getting an on-the-spot checkup from a
doctor who was a personal friend of Sherrie. Jane Briggs
hovered over Politician, making sure the medic's examination was thorough.

Gadgets returned his attention to Able Team's collection
of arms and equipment. He checked each item thoroughly,
set it aside and began fieldstripping and checking the next
piece.

Sherrie and Lyons seemed to be the only two who were
relaxed. They sat side by side on chaise longues, sipped tall

drinks that contained mostly juice and little alcohol and talked in quiet voices.

Ten feet away Nikko and Mauna Makanani sat staring at Lyons as if they expected him to hurl lightning bolts from his fingertips at any moment.

"What's got them?" Lyons asked their hostess.

"They're not accustomed to meeting gods. They'll get over it."

Lyons snorted. "They don't look that gullible."

"They're not. You are a god."

"Now don't you start."

"What's a god?" Sherrie asked. "Give me a definition that fits all the gods mankind has worshipped to date."

"First, they're immortal."

"Not always. Many cultures have mortal gods. Many gods have been entirely forgotten. What's that say about mortality?"

Lyons took another sip of his mai tai. "Gods embody larger-than-life forces," he decided.

Sherrie smiled. "That'll do. You arrive at the airport and deflect a spear from the air that was intended to kill someone. Poor Mauna goes to a sanctuary when he needs help, and who rescues him? I'd say that makes you a larger-than-life force."

"Stop it. I'm nothing but a man."

Lilivokalani looked him up and down appreciatively. "You're definitely a man."

The doctor finished his examination. "You're as fit as an eighteen-year-old," he told Blancanales. "Those burns are superficial. They'll heal in a few days. I don't see what the fuss is about."

Politician suddenly realized he was fit. He had been feeling sorry for himself because he had lost that extra edge that marked Able Team. That would come back with training. Yeah, he was fit.

Duty done, the doctor accepted a drink from Sherrie. He found a chair close to Politician, curious about what the man did for a living. There were a number of bullet scars on his body.

But before the doctor could think of a diplomatic way to start pumping his patient, Gadgets exclaimed, "What the hell is this!"

He was looking at a small gizmo in his hand that was buzzing like a bumblebee. The noise grew more frantic as Gadgets turned. He followed the buzzing to a side table in the center of the lanai. His hand swooped under the table and groped. In a moment it emerged with a black disk about the size of a fifty-cent piece but twice as thick. The disk trailed four inches of copper wire.

"What's that?" Sherrie asked.

"You've got bugs, lady," Gadgets told her.

It was not the most opportune time for Stew Williams to make an entrance. As he strode across the lawn, he shouted, "Anyone talking about me?"

"Ahh, the lord of the flies and other fine bugs," Gadgets proclaimed. "Let me mix you a CIA special."

He went over to the cart and found a tall glass and a bottle of vodka. He splashed two inches of the clear liquor into the glass.

"You start with lots of vodka, because the Russians must get their information from somewhere. Then you add a CIA cherry. Voilà! Instant détente."

Williams looked at the eavesdropping device that Gadgets had dropped into the vodka.

"What's this?"

"The latest in CIA equipment, I believe," Gadgets answered in a frosty voice. "Sherrie thought E-4 was a friend. Within the United States, too. Tell your boss he ought to be ashamed of himself."

Williams dumped the vodka into an ice bucket and retrieved the bug.

"You think I had something to do with this?"

Gadgets shrugged. "Probably not. You were too busy chasing us. Tell him to put his bugs and his cockroaches to work outside of the United States."

Williams tossed the device up and down while he eyed Gadgets. The electronics specialist's brown eyes held none of their usual laughter or warmth.

Williams went over to Lyons and returned the Python, butt first.

"The shooting's been straightened out. There were enough witnesses to make things easy."

Lyons accepted the weapon, saying only, "Thanks."

A graveyard hush fell over the lanai. Williams turned to leave.

The princess's voice stopped him. "Stew, you're welcome here, but only as a friend."

He turned back and smiled. "I'll return when the frost's out of the ground." Then he trudged back across the lawn to the parking area.

Sherrie broke the silence. "I suppose you'll be rushing back to the mainland now that you've found your friend."

Lyons shook his head.

"There's the slight problem of finding what the *spetsnaz* are really after," Politician explained.

"Oh? I was under the impression that this was some sort of a grudge match."

"They wouldn't have bothered with me if they weren't worried that I'd interfere with whatever it is they're planning. But we have no idea what they're after. The island isn't exactly brimming with strategic targets."

The princess lapsed into thought. The lanai remained silent until another car pulled into the parking area. This time it was Lao Ti who crossed the lawn.

"How does she do it?" Lilivokalani asked. "She moves as if she were on roller skates. Her shoulders don't go up and down at all."

"She had her feet amputated and driving wheels from an old steam engine grafted onto her ankles," Gadgets answered.

Lilivokalani had no patience for his inanities.

"If you can't be more humorous than that, give up," she responded.

Gadgets answered in an injured voice, "You get kicked by her in combat practice and you'll believe me."

Much to the princess's bewilderment, his comment brought laughter from the other members of Able Team. They all knew that even on the restrained level of the practice floor Lao Ti's small feet left bruises that lasted for weeks.

Lao accepted a glass of pineapple juice and sat down before reporting. "Cowley's training at a small place just north of Waimea. There's a battalion of spooks acting as security. I guess he's here to race."

"Goodness, I could have told you that," the princess murmured.

"The Russians are keeping an eye on him, anyway," Lao added.

"We'd expect them to do that," Blancanales said.

Lyons and Gadgets said nothing, although both were obviously deep in thought. The lanai was very quiet.

Gadgets looked up but waited for Ironman to speak first.

"We've got a three-cornered fight. How secure can we be electronically?" Lyons asked Gadgets.

Schwarz shook his head. "They don't need to go into our rooms. They can drive spikes into a floor, wall or ceiling and tape everything said in the next room."

"We need our own four walls," Lyons decided. He turned to Sherrie. "Can we rent a house or something?"

She laughed. "Not before the triathlon. Everything's rented six months in advance during the race. You'll simply have to stay here."

"It wouldn't be safe to dance with us," Gadgets told her. "Sometimes the music gets hot."

"Two people escaped from you at the Place of Refuge. My car was there. And where do you think you found that 'CIA cherry,' as you called it? I'd say I'm already involved. I'm also willing to bet it's safer having you people around than not having you here," the princess claimed.

Gadgets was left standing in the middle of the lanai with nothing to say.

Politician laughed. "Depends what you call safe. Ironman's a horny old goat when he's not fighting."

Lilivokalani arched an eyebrow. "Who wants to be that safe?"

Everyone laughed except Lyons. He looked uncomfortable.

"We'll stay," he decided.

Politician hastened to add, "Thank you. We'll try not to drive you insane."

"I'll work on security measures," Gadgets said.

"The rest of you move us from the hotel to here," Lyons said, standing up. Then he turned to Sherrie. "I'll be back for that feast you're lining up."

"You had better be. I'm not accustomed to throwing luaus without the guest of honor."

"Where are you going?" Blancanales asked Lyons.

"To kick E-4's ass until he pulls some strings for me."

"What sort of strings?"

"I'm entering the triathlon."

"Hey, man," Gadgets exclaimed, "entries closed months ago."

"The State Department got the Russians in."

"He's not State "

"He's CIA. They can blackmail State into anything."

"Why the sudden urge to enter the Ironman race?" Gadgets questioned.

"How else are we going to keep an eye on the *spetsnaz*?" Lyons demanded.

Sherrie threw him her car keys, and he started to leave.

"You go nowhere until I check your Python," Gadgets told him.

"Nothing wrong with the Python."

"The spooks had it."

Lyons handed over his gun.

Gadgets looked at Politician, "Bring me my magnifying glass. It's in the left pocket of my bag."

"Wait on yourself," Jane Briggs flared.

But Blancanales got up and fished around in an outside pocket of Gadgets's war bag.

"Not here."

"Shit! I must have left it behind."

"Idiot," Politician answered, and stalked out of the lanai.

Gadgets quickly fieldstripped the big Colt. Then he tossed away the ammunition and put in fresh rounds .

Lyons spent his time recharging his speed loaders.

Gadgets handed the weapon back. "Doubt they messed with it."

Lyons holstered the weapon in the small of his back and left without another word.

**12**

Puopelu Ranch proved to be more of a tourist resort than a working ranch. It was located not far from the junction of Highway 19 and Saddle Road. Ernest Cowley and his minions had taken over eight of the ranch's twelve motel units.

Lyons found Cowley by parking the princess's Mercedes next to the only other Mercedes in the lot and pounding on the door of the nearest motel unit.

The pounding brought security men rushing from each of the adjacent rooms. Lyons ignored them and continued to hammer on the door with his open palm, a short, sharp rhythm that left the entire door vibrating like a drumhead. The door was yanked open, and Cowley stood in the entrance, wearing his best glare.

In addition to the angry frown, the chief CIA briefing officer wore a bright Hawaiian sport shirt and a yellow bathing suit. Lyons took a second look at the man's pith helmet; he thought those things had gone out with silent movies. Cowley held a brown pair of pants in his hand.

"It's you," Cowley said. The tone lacked appreciation.

"Amazing deduction," Lyons answered as he shouldered past Cowley into the motel room.

The air conditioner was idle, and it was muggy. After a moment's hesitation, Cowley left the door open and proceeded to put his pants on over his bathing suit.

"I don't have time for a social call. I'm going for my training swim."

Lyons ignored the hostility in the CIA officer's voice. "I want a favor."

"Good luck."

"Get me into the Ironman Triathlon."

"You're as nutty as a fruitcake. You have to qualify months in advance, and I doubt that you'd qualify."

"The officials leave the door open to invite whoever they wish. That must be how the State Department got the Russians in."

"I'm not the State Department."

"You'll persuade them."

"Persuade whom? The State Department?"

"Whoever it takes. Just do it."

"Don't be a fool. The race is in two days. You have no time to condition or train. You'd kill yourself."

"That would break your heart, right?"

Cowley threw his hands up in a gesture of despair. He zipped up his pants before returning his attention to Lyons.

"Why this sudden urge to compete?"

"I want to know what the Russians are up to."

"Doesn't seem to be any business of yours."

"They made it my business."

Cowley sighed. "I was going to talk to you about this anyway. I think things have been blown out of proportion. We all know that a few agents travel with every team of athletes. One apparently recognized a member of your team and went overboard. They now have a number of dead men to account for. Both the Russians and State Department don't want this to reach the news media. It would destroy our efforts to improve relations between the two countries."

"How do you improve relations with people who are trying to kill you?"

"I think you lack perspective on this."

"Possibly. That often happens when someone points a gun at you."

"So why not leave it to cooler heads?"

"Okay."

Cowley couldn't believe his ears. "Okay?"

"Sure. You and State suck off the Russians. Just get me into that race."

"You know that's impossible."

Lyons turned to go out the door. As he passed Cowley, he pulled the pith helmet off the agent's head and jammed it into his pocket.

"If that's the way you want it," Lyons growled.

Alarm flared in Cowley's eyes. He was too upset to worry about his hat.

"What do you mean by that?"

"I'm placing those *spetsnaz* bastards under citizen's arrest for attempted murder. I have witnesses. It'll stick."

"State won't let you."

"State can explain that to the reporters I'm going to brief."

Cowley rolled his eyes and sighed. Why did this cold-eyed bastard have to be so irrational?

"And if you manage to enter the triathlon?"

"I'll find out what, or who, they're after. That's more important."

"Are you going to race or watch the Russians?"

"I'm going to race enough to watch the Russians. They want something."

"Only your head. I can sympathize. They obviously recognized you and jumped the gun. There are always security people accompanying their athletes. You eliminated all the security people but two. They'll pull in their horns."

"Is that their story?"

"I'll accept it. We can't risk a confrontation with the Russians right now."

Lyons said nothing.

After a strained silence, Cowley gave in. "Okay. Okay! I'll try."

Lyons shook his head.

"What's wrong now?"

"Don't try, do it."

"I'll do my best. I'll get in touch with you later today. The King Kam?"

"No. I'm staying with Sherrie."

"You're what?" Cowley shouted.

Lyons didn't bother repeating himself.

"You'll get that lady killed."

"You just said the Russians only wanted my head."

"Get out of there."

"It's too late. She was driving us in her car when we ran into the *spetsnaz* at the Place of Refuge. She's already involved. Aren't you glad they're just harmless athletes."

"Williams!" Cowley shouted.

The baby-faced operative stuck his head around the open door.

"I'm postponing my swim until I make some phone calls. Load this jerk into his car and drive him away from here. Have three of the boys follow in the Ford to drive you back from Princess Lilivokalani's. If he argues, shoot him."

Williams looked at his boss speculatively but said nothing. Then he turned to round up a crew.

"He should have made sure you didn't get in here," E-4 grumbled. "Beat it and let me get on the blower."

Lyons walked out without saying another word.

Williams opened the door of Cowley's car. Two units down the row of motel rooms, three men piled into a blue sedan.

"That's your boss's car," Lyons told Williams. "We take this one."

"They're almost the same. Simple mistake," the CIA man said somewhat sheepishly.

"Interesting, isn't it?"

Williams caught the implication in Lyon's statement. "No, sir. His family's loaded."

Lyons slid into the back seat. "So's he. Unload him and you'd fertilize the entire island."

Williams tried not to, but he had to smile.

A bakery truck challenged Williams for the exit from the motel. Williams won, but the blue Ford had to let the truck through. They took the Mamalahoa Highway south past the police station, Parker Ranch Headquarters and the Kohala Airport. Before they reached the junction with Saddle Road, two black-and-whites moved from a side road to block the highway. Williams obediently brought the Mercedes to a smooth halt.

"Fool!" Lyons barked. His Python came out of its back holster.

He was too late. Armed men jumped out of the ditch on both sides of the road. Lyons and Williams were covered by six handguns before Ironman could be absolutely certain he wasn't in a police trap. He now knew what the chart meant and what type of game the Russians had been rehearsing. He had just been tagged "it."

BLANCANALES AND GADGETS HAD WORKED together for a long time. When Gadgets asked Politician for the magnifying glass from his war bag, he didn't need a gesture or a tone of voice to catch the additional message. Pol knew Gadgets had something on his mind. When the left pocket of the bag yielded tracking devices and a small radio to pick up their directional signal, Blancanales knew what to do.

Blancanales took a route past the front door where he shamelessly pilfered a set of car keys from Nikko's bag. He then slipped out a side door and jogged around the far end of the hedge to the parking lot.

The Able Team warrior slapped a magnetic screamer onto the roof of the Mercedes where Lyons would be least likely to see it. For good luck he put another on the spare tire of Waihee's Jeep. Then he hurried out of sight seconds before Ironman reached the parking area.

Blancanales gave his teammate a good head start before taking Nikko's car. He placed the receiver on the dashboard where body metal wouldn't screen the signal from the tracking device and then started after Lyons. It was standard operating procedure to have a member of the team checking another's backtrack. Lyons rarely thought to order it for himself. Blancanales and Gadgets had found it easier to simply do it without talking about it.

When Lyons pulled into the ranch motel, Blancanales drove a quarter mile farther before he found a place to park where Ironman's sharp eyes wouldn't spot the car. Politician left the Pinto and moved closer to the motel. He watched as Ironman was escorted from the motel by Williams and three other men.

Blancanales had to run to get back to the Pinto in time to join the procession. First there was the luxury car driven by Williams with Lyons in the back. Then a delivery truck wedged itself between the Mercedes and the Ford carrying the three CIA men. The Pinto brought up the rear.

At first Politician was amused by the Ford's vain attempts to pass the meandering truck. But when he realized that the escort was falling well behind the Mercedes, a small warning light flashed.

When the truck slewed across the highway and stopped, Blancanales was out of the Pinto before the CIA operatives finished cursing the stupidity of the driver. He passed the Company Ford and ran alongside the truck. A smiling driver had already climbed out of the cab with the vehicle's keys in one hand. The Able Team warrior needed no further proof that the man intended to abandon the vehicle in the middle of the highway.

Politician was already running; the driver was only beginning to run. Before he could reach his full pace, a gun barrel was slammed into the side of his head and the keys were snatched from his hand. The driver swung around only to be jabbed in the face with the barrel of a small submachine gun.

"You want to live. Run like hell," Blancanales said.

The driver spoke Russian but little English. However, he understood the repercussions of superior firepower. He ran like hell.

By the time Blancanales swung into the truck cab, the CIA operatives had decided to investigate the truck. One opened the passenger door just as Pol started the engine. He also had the privilege of examining the dispensing end of a mini-Uzi, which Blancanales held in his left hand and pointed across his body.

The CIA agent quickly shut the door.

Pol swept the small subgun across his body and used it to bat another spook away from his door as he slammed the gearshift into low. The truck roared down the highway.

"OUT OF THE CAR," someone ordered.

"Don't move," Lyons growled at Williams.

They were surrounded by handguns. It had never occurred to Williams that anyone would refuse to recognize the persuasive power of that many weapons. But Lyons had the big Python poised to strike the Russian who had ordered them from the car. He was totally ignoring the five other guns pointed at him.

"Those things kill," Williams pointed out.

"Then why haven't they?" Lyons snapped back.

Williams's sigh indicated that he didn't find Lyons's logic very reassuring, especially when there was a gun barrel pushing against his skull.

Lyons thumbed back the hammer of the Colt. The click vibrated through the air.

"Fifteen-gram trigger pull," he told the Russian, who seemed to be involved in a staring contest with the barrel. "I go, you go."

Lyons was slouched down in the middle of the back seat. It would be impossible to grapple with him without opening a door. The Russians hesitated.

Then the roar of a truck filled their ears. Both men briefly glanced to the rear. The stolen truck that was supposed to be blocking the CIA's Ford was bearing down on them at forty miles an hour. The truck showed no signs of slowing.

Lyons kept his gun and his attention riveted on the *spetsnaz* agent. Suddenly a number of the highly trained Russian specialists ran for the ditch.

The truck barreled past the Mercedes, missing it by only inches. It slammed into one of the black-and-whites blocking the road and shoved the car thirty feet up the highway.

Lyons turned his attention to the three Russian killers standing to the right of the Mercedes. Before they could wrench their eyes from the damage caused by the truck, the Python kissed two of them goodbye. The third barely had time to drop below door level. The angry .45 that whistled through the door tagged his shirtsleeve.

"Go!" Lyons shouted at Williams.

Williams jumped his foot from the brake to the gas. The elegant car left rubber on the highway.

"Stop!" Lyons shouted almost immediately.

Williams didn't question the Able Team warrior's order. The car screeched to a halt beside the truck. Blancanales leaped from the truck and into the car amid a volley of

9 mm Russian heartstoppers. Williams didn't need to be told to step on it.

"I left Nikko's car in the middle of the road back there," Politician said.

Lyons straightened up and looked back. They were out of range. The Russian gunmen had taken off cross-country rather than stay and argue with the three CIA men in the Ford who had finally reached the scene.

"Want to go back for it?" He asked Blancanales.

"He doesn't. He doesn't," Williams shouted from the front seat. "I'll take care of it."

"Kind of you to offer," Politician told the CIA operative as he leaned back in the soft leather seat.

"This kind of cuts you out of the triathlon," he told Ironman.

"How do you figure that?"

"The Russians won't give up. Though we might have enough on them to get them sent home."

Lyons shook his head. "We need to know their target."

"You," Williams said from the front seat.

"Wouldn't bother with me if they weren't after something else."

Williams shrugged as he drove. Lyons turned his attention back to Blancanales.

"So?"

"So you'll be an easy target in that damn race. There's no way to protect you."

"Yeah," Lyons agreed. "It'll be interesting.

## 13

Lyons, Blancanales, Schwarz and Lao Ti were holding a council of war on Lilivokalani's lanai when Ernest Cowley pulled his Mercedes into the parking area. Able Team broke off and watched as E-4, followed by three bodyguards, crossed the lawn. Sherrie had taken Mauna and Nikko Makanani to retrieve their respective vehicles.

Cowley settled into a canvas deck chair. His henchmen stationed themselves at various points on the open veranda. Each man kept one hand in a jacket pocket and their eyes on the members of Able Team.

"Williams tells me you ran into some trouble on the way home," Cowley began.

Lyons had been flicking foam from the top of his beer.

"Have a drink?"

Cowley shook his head impatiently. "I'm in training."

"Anyone else?" Ironman asked the bodyguards.

They stared straight ahead, pretending they hadn't heard him.

"When the boss trains, they all train," Gadgets suggested.

"About the trouble," Cowley insisted.

"No trouble."

"No trouble? No trouble!" Cowley's voice rose a half octave. "You've left the bodies of half a dozen foreign nationals littering the island since you arrived—men who are here because the government interceded with the triathlon committee. And, for some reason that I can't fathom, Williams seems compelled to clean up your messes for you.

"Now we have Moscow on the hot line screaming at the President. The President has the director's tail in a sling. And guess who the director's leaning on?"

"Do you have my entry forms?" Lyons asked.

Cowley stared at Lyons. The CIA briefing officer couldn't believe his ears. He took a deep breath.

"You think we're going to put you in the same race with people you're shooting right, left and center?"

Gadgets butted in with, "I don't think the *spetsnaz* would appreciate the 'right' part of that question. They don't mind being called 'left,' and you might get away with 'center,' but not 'right.'

Cowley glared at Schwarz. "Who let you in?"

"If you're going to be a spook, you should really get this left and right business straight," Gadgets answered.

Cowley pivoted to look at Blancanales and Lao. "Is anyone here sane?"

"The Ironman entry?" Lao Ti asked in a cold voice.

"No chance now."

Lyons stood up suddenly, causing a ripple of unease among the bodyguards.

"Time for the police," he said.

"The police?"

"Sure," Lyons told Cowley. "I know of at least two incidents of attempted murder. We're going to file complaints."

"I had a little talk with the police. They won't listen."

Lyons shrugged. "When we swear our complaints, they're forced to follow through. And there's also the press. I'm amazed that they haven't picked up on this yet."

Cowley sighed. "What do you really want?"

"To know what the *spetsnaz* are after. We know enough to send them home, but the politicians wouldn't like it. Besides, what's on this island that's worth the effort?"

"You," Cowley answered. "They've tried for you twice. They may succeed next time."

"He wouldn't be here if the *spetsnaz* hadn't been chasing me already," Blancanales pointed out. "Whatever they're after was already on the island. They just figure we're trying to get in the way."

"I told you it was just a couple of them out for revenge."

"And again today? Come off it," Blancanales said.

"Why don't you leave this for the FBI?"

Lyons was not going to waste any more time. He headed for the parking area.

"Stop him," Cowley told his bodyguards. He whipped out a .357 Magnum and ordered the rest of Able Team to stay put.

"As long as we don't miss the show," Gadgets told him.

The three CIA henchmen took off as if they were hounds let loose for the hunt. They sprinted across the grass, catching up to Lyons just as he reached the pool. He strode straight ahead, ignoring them.

When the first hand fell on Lyons's left shoulder, he seized it in his right hand and pivoted, forcing the agent to spin 180 degrees. An easy punch to the kidney sent him staggering into a colleague.

The third man found himself facing Lyons on a one-to-one basis. The CIA operative knew he was outmanned, but he didn't back off. Lyons would probably send him to the hospital, but Cowley would send him to Central America if he didn't attempt to stop the Able Team warrior.

Lyons used one of Lao Ti's techniques. He stepped to one side and grabbed an outflung arm. Using his body as a fulcrum, he redirected the CIA man's charge and sent him crashing into both of his friends.

Before the three men could fully recover, each was pushed into the shallow end of the pool. They stood sputtering, knee-high in decorative lilies. One went for his gun.

"Enough," Cowley roared, but he was too late.

Lyons's boot flashed. The Colt automatic did a small arc and landed in the deep end of the pool. Lyons didn't have to produce a weapon—the other two agents raised their arms.

E-4 was so unnerved by how easily his bodyguards had been taken out of action that he scarcely noticed when Gadgets plucked the small automatic from his grasp.

Lyons strode back to the lanai, herding the bodyguards ahead of him like three wet sheep.

When he reached the house, he bellowed at Cowley, "You've got one hour to get that entry, or these three face charges, too. The press would like to hear about their armed operations on American soil."

Cowley examined Lyons's face for ten seconds and decided he wasn't bluffing. He strode back to his car without another word, leaving his shamefaced muscle behind.

Twenty-five minutes later two cars and a Jeep pulled in and Sherrie, Jane, Nikko and Mauna joined Able Team and three embarrassed CIA men. No one questioned the presence of the three men who were obviously CIA. The unwilling guests finally accepted drinks. Able Team continued to go over the race route and to plan security.

Fifty-five minutes later Cowley telephoned to say that he was still trying to get the entry approved. Lyons made him sweat five minutes before agreeing to wait one more hour before informing the press.

Lyons hung up the telephone and looked at the crowd that had collected on the lanai.

"I'll get an entry," he told Able Team. "Let's go somewhere and plan."

Lao Ti stood up. Blancanales and Gadgets stayed in their chairs. Lyons sat down again.

"What's eating you two?"

"You really want to kill yourself?" Gadgets asked.

Lyons let his disgust show. "I'm there to watch the *spetsnaz*."

Blancanales shook his head. "We know you. You'll get swept up in the race. Can you take it?"

Lyons opened his mouth, then closed it again. He thought about their question.

Able Team didn't interrupt. Lyons was deficient in many departments such as tact, diplomacy and communication but the rest of the team could work with him because he didn't believe in self-deception. Once his nose was rubbed in the issue, he would give an honest answer.

"I can keep up," Lyons decided. "Can't win. Won't try. When they make their move, it'll be up to you three."

Gadgets and Blancanales exchanged glances as they stood up. They had their answer. The die was cast. No one said it would take a miracle to keep Lyons alive. No one said it, but Schwarz, Blancanales and Lao Ti all thought it. There were the rigors of the race. Lyons couldn't set his own pace; he would have to stay close to the Russians. The Russians might decide to take him out. It would be impossible to screen all of their attempts. And would the CIA be friend or foe?

Instead of leading them into the house, Lyons moved the group onto the lawn and into the shade of the smokethorn trees. From there they could watch for unexpected arrivals and keep an eye on their CIA guests. A half hour of poring over maps and discussing contingency plans followed.

One hour and fifty-two minutes after his quick exit, Cowley was back with a letter approving Carl Lyons as a special entry in the race. A sheath of forms was attached. He delivered the documents without saying a word and motioned for his bodyguards to follow him. They seemed almost reluctant to leave their lounge chairs and their drinks.

"I'm not through with you," Lyons told Cowley.

E-4 managed a smile. "You have some last request? You're going to kill yourself in that race, you know. It takes months of conditioning."

"You're taking me shopping."

"Huh?"

"Bring your muscle if you like. I need to be outfitted You're the only expert I know "

"Just go to a sporting goods store and buy cheap. You won't live to use anything a second time. You have no idea what that heat and those winds are like," Cowley declared

Lyons's smile was edged in frost. "Then it's a good thing you'll be there to tell me what I need for those special con ditions."

"I'm supposed to be training."

"So am I. You're wasting our time."

Cowley motioned to his men, saying, "Let's get this over with."

They took Lyons to Kona's largest sporting goods store. If the clerk found it strange that three large men fanned through the store before two others came into the shop, he gave no sign of it. He homed in on Cowley, who obviously knew what he wanted.

Cowley told him. "This man needs to be outfitted for the Ironman."

"Clothing for which part?"

"Clothing and equipment for everything. But keep it cheap. He won't live to use anything a second time."

"We'd better take the events in order. First the swim. You have your own trunks of course?" the clerk asked as he directed them to the far side of the store.

Lyons shook his head.

"We have some excellent . . ."

"Give him a one-piece triathlon suit," Cowley interrupted. "Saves changing time."

"They're excellent for swimming and running, but they bind on the bicycle," the slim storekeeper pointed out.

"Where do you change?" Lyons asked.

"Changing tents are provided at each stage of the race. There'll be volunteers to help you with sunscreen lotion," Cowley answered.

Lyons knew that changing was out. He intended to hide a weapon somewhere on his body.

"The one-piece," he told the clerk.

"That's not a good choice for cycling."

"The one-piece."

The clerk produced an outfit that looked like a singlet sewn to the top of a pair of shorts.

Ironman took it and marched to a changing room. Cowley and the clerk discussed the other items Lyons would need while he tried on the suit. Two minutes later he appeared in the doorway.

"A good fit," the clerk admitted.

"Looser in the thighs," Lyons demanded.

"It's meant to be like that so it won't ride up."

"Looser."

"We have a suit designed for overweight men, but it's of really inferior material."

"That one looks about right," Cowley commented.

"No, it's got to be looser."

The clerk sighed and went for another one-piece.

Lyons tried it. It wasn't much better, but it would hide a flat knife taped to the thigh. It would be his only chance to carry a weapon. The main problem with clothing that was light enough to prevent heat prostration was that it didn't make allowances for concealing weapons.

"I'll take it," he told the clerk when he emerged five minutes later.

"No, he won't," Cowley interrupted. "Find him one with a pocket on the back."

The clerk retreated once more, and Cowley explained the choice to Lyons. "You have to eat during the bike race. The organizers distribute oranges and bananas every five miles, but you need a steady supply of energy."

The clerk brought back another garment. It was one piece also, but the back was doubled, acting as a huge pocket.

When Lyons emerged from the change room, Cowley was barely able to stifle a laugh. The suit was meant for an overweight, non-athletic man. It hung on Lyons. The Able Team warrior made a series of twisting and stretching moves. The suit didn't bind; it barely stayed on.

"Perfect," Lyons said.

He didn't return to the change room but finished the shopping in the baggy sportswear.

The clerk repressed a shudder and asked, "Goggles?"

"You'll need them to protect your eyes," Cowley added.

Lyons shook his head. He didn't have time to get used to them. Besides, they would be a handicap in a fight.

"If you're not going to take my advice, I'd better get back to training," Cowley grumbled.

"Stay," Lyons answered.

"You'll need Vaseline for the swim and a sunscreen for the bike race and run," the clerk said.

Lyons nodded. He had learned while in Central America that his fair skin required complete sunscreen protection.

The clerk produced the two small items, then smiled. "Do you need a bicycle?" he asked.

Lyons nodded.

"We have all of the best Italian and Japanese frames," he boasted as he led the way across the store.

"Forget the handmade stuff," Cowley said. "He's killing himself. He may as well do it on the cheap models."

The clerk sighed at the thought of the lost sale. "This isn't a bad cycle for the price," he said, taking an assembled frame from a rack.

Cowley sniffed. "He's going to be in enough pain without getting a hernia as well. Give him good wheels with tubular tires and chrome moly tubing."

Lyons stood and watched as the clerk put together a cycle under Cowley's guidance. The half-inch wide tires had to be glued onto the wheel rims.

"Those things won't hold me up," he protested.

"They will when inflated to 120 pounds," Cowley told him.

"They'll hold 120 pounds of pressure?"

The clerk nodded.

"I want a pump on the frame," Lyons said.

"Don't be silly," Cowley snapped. "You don't fix flats in a race, and you don't use a hand pump to reach 120 pounds."

"A pump," Lyons insisted.

The clerk sighed even louder and attached a clamp for a pump.

"It will be nearly a pound heavier," he said.

When the cycle was finally assembled, it was put on a roller bed for Lyons to try. He had to make a couple of attempts before he caught on to the idea of balancing without moving forward. He ran the twelve-speed through its gears.

"Higher gears," he decided.

"You don't know those winds," Cowley said. "Stay with those gears."

Lyons shook his head. He was used to long treks with heavy packs. He knew that he couldn't pedal as fast as the trained athletes, but he could pedal harder.

"I suppose I could put on a block intended for a three-speed crank set," the clerk said, his voice dubious.

Cowley nodded.

The next attempt on the roller frame suited Lyons. It felt more like the heavy resistance of an exercise cycle.

"I'll take it. What's next?"

"Helmet, gloves, socks and shoes," the clerk mumbled.

"Don't need the fancy junk. Just the essentials."

Cowley exploded. "They *are* essentials, you ass. Hard helmets are required. You could use the same shoes for biking and running, but soft soles would absorb a lot of the force you apply to the pedals. But we'll go with lined shoes. He doesn't want to waste time on socks."

"No gloves," Lyons said, not wanting to be hampered if he needed to shoot. He hadn't written off the possibility of taking a gun.

The clerk found a pair of blue shoes. The baggy triathlon suit was green. The helmet, which Lyons had chosen for maximum size and the extension that acted as a sun visor, was red. The Ironman looked as if he was set to be the comic relief in the race.

"And now we need a bottle and dried food," Cowley said.

The clerk was glad of a chance to leave them. He came back with a plastic bottle and another clip for the frame of the bicycle.

"Put on three," Lyons told the clerk. "And I'll take figs with me."

"You don't need three clips. You can leave spare bottles with the committee and pick them up along the route," Cowley explained.

"Okay. Six bottles, two clips and plenty of Gatorade."

"You have to get used to it," Cowley said.

"I am."

Fitting Lyons for the run wasn't any easier. Cowley insisted on the best shoes in the store, shouting down Lyons's objections that it felt like running on sponges. The clerk attempted to sell them another outfit without success. Lyons chose a sun visor and then bought some glue and glued a handkerchief to the band to shade his neck, a sensible idea that did nothing to enhance his ludicrous appearance.

"You'll need reflective tape for the run," the clerk announced. "It's part of the rules." His tone of voice challenged the two men to question him.

Cowley answered in a mild voice, "Don't you think you should throw that in? We're spending quite a bit of money here."

The clerk didn't want to argue. He produced a couple of rolls.

"Do I have to wear this?" Ironman asked, thinking it would make him even more of a target.

He applied the tape to the shorts and to the shoes, hoping the lowness of the target would cause evening snipers to misjudge the distance. The decoration did nothing to make his outfit look in the least bit dignified.

"That seems to cover everything," the clerk sighed.

"What about a knapsack?" Lyons said as he changed back to the cycling shoes.

The clerk didn't question the request; he merely found the required item and then started to ring in the sales. As he waited to pay the bill, Lyons dropped the items, including his street clothes, into the sack.

"I'll ride the bike back to Sherrie's," he told Cowley.

"You're through with me?"

Lyons nodded.

Cowley left the store, followed by his escort.

The clerk stopped Lyons as he started to wheel the cycle out of the store. "We could deliver everything this afternoon," he suggested.

"I'll ride home."

"One favor, please."

Lyons was surprised. He looked at the clerk and waited for him to continue.

"If someone asks who outfitted you, would you please give the name of one of our competitors?"

"You did okay."

When Ironman rode his bike up to the lanai half an hour later, Blancanales was the first to react. "Is this what the well-dressed target is wearing this season?"

"Yeah," Gadgets cracked, "but who's going to get him first, the *spetsnaz* or the CIA?"

Not even Gadgets laughed. The question hit too close to home.

## 14

"What's been happening?" Lyons asked.

"We found more bugs, and we're taking countermeasures."

Lyons raised an eyebrow.

"We transferred the electronic tail from Sherrie's car to E-4's. I put a small ear in the back seat just before you went shopping. When we know he's out, we'll go for the motel."

"He's not the enemy."

"You sure?"

Lyons shook his head. "Just a feeling."

"Strong enough to call us off?" Blancanales asked.

Lyons shook his head again. "Where's everyone else?" he asked.

"Lao went for electronic and diving supplies. The rest are helping Sherrie prepare for the feast in your honor, Mr. God," Gadgets told him.

"Shut up," Lyons growled.

Blancanales and Gadgets glanced at each other. Lyons caught them at it.

"I'm not a god, but don't make fun of their customs," Lyons warned. "They're good people."

"Excuse us!" Gadgets shouted. "He's just proved them wrong by showing the first signs of humanity."

Lyons glared but said nothing. Politician got up and slapped him on the back. It was a sign of approval that Lyons needed. The Ironman turned and walked away.

"Time to train," he said over his shoulder.

THE ELECTRONIC SUPPLY HOUSE was busy. While waiting to be served, Lao Ti amused herself by listening to the parts being requested and imagining the project or repair being undertaken. The exercise kept her occupied until a clerk had time to wait on her. Silently she handed him her shopping list.

Another clerk started to assemble parts for two men wearing lightweight suits. They were standing just down the counter from Lao, and their nasal midwestern twang carried easily. Their purchases jolted her; they were the same type of supplies she was ordering for Gadgets.

Lao hastily put her purchases into the back of Nikko's small wagon, slid behind the wheel and waited. Ten minutes later the two men emerged from the shop. The man with the box of parts went in one direction. The other came toward her.

Before she could select a course of action, someone stepped from the car parked behind her and approached her window. He leaned down as if he were engaged in a friendly conversation and pointed a Smith & Wesson No. 39 automatic between her eyes. The man from the store slid into the front seat beside her.

He turned to look at the box in the back of the wagon. "Let's go where we can have a quiet talk about those supplies."

He produced another Smith & Wesson, covering her while his companion slid into the back seat. A moment later the other man from the store joined them. He set his box of electronic parts next to Lao's and then turned to look at the small Oriental.

"One of us had better drive," he told Lao. "My friend will get out and walk around the car. You keep your hands where we can see them as you slide over."

Lao stayed where she was, saying nothing.

The man who was supposed to drive appeared at the door and growled, "Move over."

Lao looked straight ahead as if she hadn't heard anything. After a tense fifteen seconds, the man outside the car bent down to discuss the situation with his two colleagues in the back.

Lao's hand flew to the door handle, and her shoulder hit the door. The edge of it caught the shoulder of the man on the outside and sent him spinning.

Lao Ti rolled low. No bullets followed her. It was the main street of Hilo, and the CIA operatives didn't want any publicity.

Lao clipped the staggering agent in the knee, and he fell against the car. A chop to the shoulder numbed his entire arm. He recovered to find himself staring into the barrel of his own automatic.

The other two agents started to scramble from the back seat. Lao threw herself against the nearest door, pinning the leg of one of the men between the door and the car. Her victim yelped in pain. She slammed the borrowed automatic into the trapped man's hand, knocking another automatic loose, then she leaped back, covering both unarmed men and keeping the car between herself and the man who still had his weapon.

"Throw it down or I'll start shooting," she said. "I can plead self-defense. You can't."

"There's been a misunderstanding . . ." one began.

She cut him off by firing a shot into the air.

The last operative tossed his weapon over the car.

Lao stood back and motioned for the three men to back toward the curb. They did so, slowly, cautiously. People were clearing the street. A patrolman was drawing his own weapon as he approached the scene.

Lao Ti tossed the confiscated weapon back to the owner, stepped into the car and drove away. In her rearview mirror, she could see the three embarrassed men being held at gunpoint by an angry police officer. She had ended up with two sets of equipment. Not bad for ninety seconds work.

Lao's next stop was a diving shop.

The owner was delighted to fill her peculiar order. She required two Poseidon fifty-cubic-foot tanks, which had higher pressure and were much smaller than most tanks. Lao Ti also ordered a good regulator, a mask, the fins right off the display and two bang sticks.

There were no questions when she bought all eight of the Tekna knives in stock. The handles of the weapons were no fatter than the blades. But when she demanded the blue tropical-weight diving suit in his display window, the owner balked.

"Makes a great window display," he told her, "but you don't want to dive in it. Blue's the wrong color for these waters. You'd disappear thirty feet away."

Lao Ti didn't argue. She turned and headed for the door.

"Hey! What about these things," he said, indicating the pile of gear on the counter.

"No suit. I'll go somewhere else. I'm small and hard to fit. I like that one."

The owner had to admit that the display sample was about the right size. The blue leotardlike suit had been made for a smaller-than-normal mannequin. The small male figure was broad in the chest, narrow in the waist and had muscular legs. It would fit the small woman beautifully.

"Okay. Seventy bucks."

She returned, not bothering to argue about the inflated price.

"One more thing," she told him.

"What? My pants?"

"They wouldn't fit," she answered seriously. "They're too big for me, and too small for you."

The two locked hostile glances.

"What else do you need?" the shopkeeper asked.

"I want to rent a DPV with its own air supply."

"Hell, lady, a diver propulsion vehicle's professional gear. You won't find anything like that here."

Lao smiled for the first time. "I couldn't find one, but you could. If you can work out a deal, I'll deposit the cost of the vehicle."

"What do you want it for?" he asked, his curiosity aroused.

She winked. "I don't want anyone to know the exact location of my dive."

"You've dived for treasure before," he concluded.

"I can afford your prices."

He laughed again. "I'll see what I can do. Where can I get in touch with you?"

"Leave a message with Princess Lilivokalani."

The answer sobered him. Doing this favor could lead to profitable business.

"I'll find it," he promised.

Lao paid him and then tore a hundred-dollar bill in half.

"Deliver it, and the rest of the finder's fee is yours."

"You got it," he answered.

After Lao left the store, the owner made a telephone call.

"The woman you described was here," he told the person on the other end. "She bought scuba gear and wants to rent a DPV."

He listened for a while, then answered, "I'll let you know."

MAJOR JAROSLAV OCIPOVICH was not grinning at Friedrich Vorovski. The small political commissar was justified in his heavy sarcasm. Ocipovich's *spetsnaz* had failed to kidnap the target, and he had lost seven more men. He fought to keep his face expressionless as Vorovski heaped abuse on him.

"There you sit," Vorovski sneered, "as if you were on vacation. Since we last talked, you have lost a third of your men. You did not corner the gray-haired American, but you lost four men trying it. You did not catch the native guide. Instead, you lost another of your men. And the kidnapping was a shambles. Two more died there. You are America's secret weapon."

"We have the backup plan," Ocipovich said.

"Wrong, comrade. I have the backup plan. You have nothing but defeat and disgrace. Any moment now, the FBI will knock on this door and take you away. It is a wonder the Americans did not arrest you long ago."

The *spetsnaz* leader stroked the blond stubble on his chin. His hand moved jerkily, his only sign of nervousness.

"If the Americans were going to arrest me, why have they not done so. We have kept the team in the open. The men have been doing their usual training routines."

"I hope you have been doing those routines faithfully, because the athletes must now compete until they can grab the target."

"We are ready to compete," Ocipovich said, his voice cold. "We are always in training."

"Good. Now all that remains is to get the authorities off our backs."

"I have seen no indication that they are on our backs." Ocipovich was sweating. He could now see where the conversation was leading.

"Why do you think that is, comrade?" The political officer's voice was far too mild.

"They do not have any proof," Ocipovich snapped. "In America authorities are expected to have solid evidence before they make an arrest."

"Do not lecture me in basic politics, comrade. If there had been no intervention, the police would have been here days ago. They are waiting to find out what our entire plan is, and who is supplying the information. Otherwise they would simply remove our target from the race."

"He is stubborn. He will not allow himself to be pulled from the race."

"Bah! He may be stubborn, but I doubt he wants to race enough to come to Mother Russia with us. I think they are trying to turn the tables on us. He is probably only here as bait for a trap."

"Are you suggesting we give up?" Ocipovich demanded.

"Hardly. I suggest you try thinking for a change. Or have all your brains been trained out of you?"

"You are living dangerously, comrade "

"Bah, I am not the one the Americans will be watching. You are the bungler. But no more. I will give the orders from now on."

Ocipovich raised a blond eyebrow. "How will you convince the others that you are now in charge? And you can bring the gun out of your pocket. I know you have been pointing it at me since you came into the room."

The small, dark Russian extracted a French-made Manurhin PPK automatic from his jacket pocket, keeping it pointed at the GRU agent.

"I wish to make sure you do not act foolishly. Your record for intelligent action has been terrible so far."

"So what do you wish me to do? Confess to the Americans and take the pressure off the rest of you?"

"I thought of it. But it would not work. Your confession would not be believed without details, and details would alert them to the plan. No, you must proceed with the race, but confine your job to screening the subject from his protection. I will see that he is scooped up."

There was a period of silence before Ocipovich asked, "And in return for giving you the glory of actually capturing this dreaded American?"

"You get the credit of cooperating freely with me despite the mess you have made."

"Not much of an offer."

"You do not have much choice."

"All right. I will enter the race as a replacement on the Russian unit. That will give us nine athletes and eleven support crew. How many of these do you wish?"

"I will tell you who I need and when."

"And you, Comrade Vorovski? You are sure you can manage to abduct the American who has managed to elude us thus far?" the big *spetsnaz* asked with a grin.

"Absolutely certain," the small commissar answered.

Something in his voice made Ocipovich shiver.

## 15

"Did you have any trouble?" Gadgets asked Lao Ti when she returned

"No trouble."

She put the two boxes of parts on the patio table in front of the electronics specialist. Gadgets looked from one box to the other and then looked up at Lao.

"What's this?"

"Two-for-one sale."

"Ironman!" Gadgets bellowed.

Lyons stopped doing calisthenics long enough to growl, "What now?"

"Lao came back with an extra box of parts. You've got all the energy. You get the story out of her."

Lyons cocked an eyebrow at Lao.

"Some of Cowley's men were buying parts at the same time I was. We had a difference of opinion, and I ended up with both sets," Lao reported.

Lyons looked at Gadgets.

"It will do to make broadcasting microphones. I'd find the stuff easily every time," Schwarz reported.

"Will it change your plans?" Lyons asked.

"I have your description of the motel. It just refines my plans."

"After this, talk to each other," Lyons muttered as he returned to his exercises.

Gadgets and Lao frowned at each other, but their eyes were laughing.

"Need any help?" Lao asked.

He nodded. She pulled a chair over to the table. It was already littered with tools.

Gadgets leaned back and thought for a moment, puffing his cheeks in and out like a lovesick frog. A smile slowly crept over his face.

He asked Lao, "If I patched you into a telephone line, could you intercept calls only to a given list of numbers?"

"Easy."

"Pol," Gadgets shouted.

Blancanales got up from where he was sitting with his arm around Jane and came over. "You sure know when to disturb a guy."

"Do we have enough money to buy a computer?"

Blancanales reached into his pocket and pulled out a bankroll. Most of Able Team's money went straight to Pol because he was the only one who could make it last. He peeled bills from his roll until Lao nodded, and then returned to his seat. Lao took the money and went back to the car.

"Jane," Gadgets shouted.

Both Blancanales and Jane Briggs looked angrily in his direction. Jane's hair was still dyed black. Her skin still looked like a Hawaiian's, although it was a bit pale in two places.

"Are you trying to drive us nuts?" she demanded. "I've been trying to tell Rosario something all day and you keep interrupting."

"Just jealous. Can you make me an appointment and take me to the place where you got your beauty treatment?"

"Take you?"

Gadgets looked genuinely desperate. "You wouldn't expect me to go to a place like that alone!"

Jane's anger dissolved into laughter. "How soon?"

"Not today. Early tomorrow."

Jane Briggs was still chuckling when she went to find the telephone.


GADGETS WORE HIS SAFARI SUIT when Lao Ti drove him to the Puopelu Ranch Motel. It was 8:30 P.M. when she stopped down the road and turned off the ignition of the rented Ford.

"Just wait," Gadgets told her "No need to intervene unless the party gets rough."

He let himself out of the car and walked toward the souvenir shop. At the last moment he changed course, putting the shop between himself and the motel.

Lao scanned the area once again. The two men lounging by the pool were studying her. They were probably CIA lookouts. She settled back in the seat and watched the row of motel rooms from the corner of her eye.

Three minutes later a shadow moved among the shadows of gathering twilight that danced across the roof. Gadgets had slipped through the lookouts and was already at work. He moved cautiously across the flat roof; the Able Team warrior had no intention of making a sound that would alert the motel occupants below. Gadgets's first goal was the motel's television dish antenna.

First he attached a black pack to the base. It contained sophisticated monitoring equipment, a voice-activated tape recorder and a sending unit that would do a high-speed dump of the material on the tape when it received a coded radio signal. There was another piece in the pack that would send an interference signal. It could also be turned on and off with radio pulses.

He stripped the lead from the dish and then quickly spliced it and attached it to the input and output of the pack. The television service was interrupted for less than twenty seconds. He doubted that anyone in the motel would notice. Gadgets ran a single strand of wire up the outside of the dish to act as an aerial. Then he covered everything with duct tape, which served as perfect camouflage for the pack.

Gadgets gave his complicated homemade device an affectionate pat and stole across the roof toward the office. The motel sign was on, but it was still not dark enough to draw a great deal of attention. Gadgets sprang from the corner of the roof to the pole that brought in the motel's telephone line. He shinnied up to the junction box. It was in an exposed position and anyone looking up could see what he was doing.

The motel office was almost directly in Lao Ti's line of vision. When she saw Gadgets leap to the telephone pole, she reached into the glove compartment and produced a cheap camera that she had borrowed from Princess Lilivokalani. She aimed it at the motel and clicked the shutter. By the time she had advanced it to the next frame, the two men by the pool were moving.

She clicked the camera twice again before the two men appeared at the car window.

"What are you doing, miss?" one asked in a calm voice.

"I'm pointing an empty camera at the motel and clicking the shutter," Lao answered. Her voice implied that it was the most natural thing in the world to do.

"Don't be smart," the other bodyguard snarled.

"Why not?"

The snarly one tried to grab the camera, but Lao pulled it away.

"You're blocking the view," Lao told him.

He swiped again. This time he had his knuckles rapped by the camera he was trying to grab.

"You two are annoying," Lao warned him.

Both operatives grabbed at once. One managed to snag Lao Ti's wrist long enough for the other to grab the camera. He immediately popped open the back.

"Hey! It *is* empty," he exclaimed.

The other agent glanced at the camera in surprise. Lao took the opportunity to unlatch the car door, and then she put the full force of her shoulder against it. She sent the two men staggering. By the time they recovered, she was standing beside the car.

"Give me back my camera," she demanded in a voice that was loud enough to carry across the street.

"What are you up to?" one bodyguard demanded.

"Police!" Lao shouted.

Another bodyguard emerged from the motel to see what was happening.

"What are you up to?" the gruff one repeated.

Lao answered by stamping on his instep. She grabbed the camera when he started hopping in pain. Instinctively the other man pulled the camera away from her again. It had to mean something.

Lao's distraction was working. It had given Gadgets the time to work slowly and calmly at the telephone line box. He had to find an unused line and convert it to the motel's primary outgoing line. It wasn't a complicated job, but it couldn't be rushed.

The operative dropped Lao's camera when the Able Team warrior kicked him in the shins. She grabbed for it as it was about to hit the pavement.

"Someone call the police," she shouted.

The door of the motel office opened, and a woman looked out.

"These men are attacking me," Lao shouted to her.

"They couldn't be. They're guests here," the motel manager called back. Then she closed the office door again.

Another motel unit opened, and two more CIA supermen came to join the game.

"Keep it down," one warned as he crossed the street.

Lao Ti eluded their attempt to retrieve the camera, but was now cornered by the four men who towered over her small form as she stood erect with her back to the car.

"I'm going to scream," she warned them.

"Shit," a newcomer said. "What's in the camera anyway."

"Not a thing," Lao told him. "These thugs grabbed it from me and opened it. It's empty."

Gadgets finally found the needed line and made the connection. He than rang through to Lilivokalani's and gave Blancanales the number. Then he closed the junction box and shinnied down the pole. It was time to take the heat off Lao.

The penetration specialist moved quickly and quietly. One CIA guard had had enough sense to stay at his post behind the motel, but his ears were trained on the loud voices coming from the front. Gadgets slid by him unnoticed.

The electronics and penetration genius crossed to the front of the motel and took five quick strides to the unit Cowley occupied.

He pounded on the door and started shouting, "Cowley, call your stooges off."

The effect was immediate, proving that Cowley had been aware of the disturbance. He yanked the door open just as a fifth man joined the group around Lao.

"Hey," the newcomer shouted loudly enough for Gadgets to hear. "This is one of the people the boss wanted us to watch out for."

But no one paid any attention. The rest of the bodyguards were running back across the street to apprehend Gadgets.

Cowley groaned. "I should have known it would be you people. What do you want?"

Another CIA operative emerged from a unit. When he saw Lao, he shouted, "That's her. That's the woman who stole our parts."

Lao's amused voice came back, heavy with phony sympathy, "Is the poor man missing his parts?"

"Okay, okay," Cowley shouted. "Back off, everyone. There's no threat." He turned to Gadgets and spoke in a lower voice. "What do you want? Other than to make my men look stupid, that is?"

"Carl just thought we owed you a favor in return for getting him into the race. So we're testing your security." Gadgets paused and shook his head sadly. "Too bad. Really too bad. Tomorrow, we'll return your bugging supplies by planting them on you."

Stew Williams had approached as Gadgets was speaking. He asked, "Why are you making us look like clowns?"

"Just thought we'd help out," Gadgets replied in an innocent voice. "Can't be too careful with E-4."

Then Gadgets strolled back to the car, whistling.

"Sweep the place for bugs," Cowley ordered one of his men.

"We did it an hour ago."

"Do it again," Cowley shouted, then slammed the door to his motel unit.

Gadgets and Lao climbed into the car, ignoring the poisonous stares from the men. Lao waved to the bodyguards and drove away

GADGETS AND JANE BRIGGS LEFT the house early the next morning. The women at the beauty parlor fondly remembered Jane's generous tips and had agreed to come in early to look after her shy gentleman.

"So I lied about the gentleman part," Jane told Gadgets.

A handsome man with short brown hair and a mustache entered the beauty shop. He wore a leisure suit and smartly shining combat boots.

An hour later Jane distributed generous tips once again, and a Hawaiian couple emerged from the shop. The female was Jane Briggs, who had obviously had the skin dye evened out.

The male Hawaiian had a droopy white mustache and short white hair. His skin was dark and his face wrinkled. He dragged his left foot slightly when he walked, and his shoulders were rounded.

The old man wore jeans that had been washed and rewashed until they were now a pale blue except for the knees, which were a well-worn white. He wore a green work shirt that was too baggy for him. Around his neck hung eight strands of seashell beads. The Hawaiian's sandals were run down at the heel.

"You sure did a lot of fanny-patting for an old man," Jane complained.

The old man leered at her. His teeth were discolored.

"Just part of the role," Gadgets said.

"Like hell," Jane muttered. Then she grudgingly admitted, "You really do look and act differently. It's hard to believe it's really you."

"It isn't. That's the whole secret. From now on I'm Hau'oli, dirty old man and TV repairman *extraordinaire*."

To prove his point, he patted her fanny. She dug an elbow into his ribs, causing him to wheeze and gasp so heavily that it took her a moment to realize it was only an act.

"I'm not sure I'll be sad if they catch you," she told him.

Gadgets turned serious. "They'll have a good chance. The whole group of them will see me up close."

## 16

Gadgets Schwarz sat in a rented van down the road from the Puopelu Ranch Motel. It was almost 8:30 the evening after his makeover. He checked the turnip watch he had hanging among his many layers of beads. His right hand rested on a small radio communicator hidden in an old tool bag on the seat beside him. When the watch read 8:30, Gadgets pushed the button.

Two minutes later the manager went to the nearest motel room. She quickly returned to the office.

At 8:38 P.M. his communicator buzzed, and Lao told him that she had intercepted the service call. It had been to Master TV Service. He waited a few minutes and then started the van and drove into the parking lot. He picked up the old tool bag and sauntered into the office, his left foot dragging slightly.

"Master TV," he told her as he leered across the counter.

She frowned. "Where's John?"

"Master couldn't come  He sent me." Gadgets laughed, spraying the desk.

She hesitated, then decided that any repairman was better than dealing with angry guests.

"Something's wrong with the antenna. There's interference on all of the screens." She turned on the office set. "Like that."

Gadgets looked at the screen for thirty seconds as if it made sense to him.

"Are all the screens the same?"

"That's what I just said."

"No one said anything about working on them damn dishes. Just said the television set. Either you got an interfering motor in the line of sight or one of the receivers is making this mess and sending it over the lines. Where's the dish?"

"On the roof."

"I didn't plan on being no bird."

The manager let out a sigh of impatience. "It's a flat roof. We've got a good ladder."

Gadgets hesitated and then sighed. "Guess I'd better have a look," he conceded reluctantly.

The woman helped him with the aluminum ladder. He reached the dish but stayed for less than five minutes.

"Nothin' wrong up there. You got a defective set contaminating the network."

"Can you find it?"

"Sure I can find it," he snapped. "We'll start with the one in the office. Just a minute."

He shuffled out to the truck and returned with a small television set. He plugged it in, took the leads off the office set and put the wires on the portable. The small screen showed nothing but snow.

"Not this one," he announced.

Then came the slow progress down the line of motel units. At each one, the manager would knock, apologize and then usher the repairman into the room. The old Hawaiian would hobble in with his open tool bag. He would leer at any woman in sight before turning his attention to the television set. Then he would disconnect the set from the aerial and try the small portable. Interference was the only thing showing on the portable.

Gadgets would mumble, "Not this damn one either," and reconnect the motel set.

The procedure continued until they came to the first unit occupied by Cowley's group. There was no one in the room, but Gadgets insisted on doing the test as the manager stood glowering in the doorway.

"The interference is much stronger on this set," Gadgets reported.

Before the manager could object, he took the back off the set and installed a bug. It was unlikely to be detected by a sweep because the microphone used little power and it didn't broadcast.

"It's just a worn condenser," Gadgets reported. "It's not the cause of the problem."

He gave the next set a clean bill of health to avoid suspicion.

The next unit was Cowley's. Gadgets shuffled a bit slower, wondering if he would pass scrutiny. Although Able Team had done well in the last several encounters against Cowley's men, Gadgets didn't underestimate their intelligence.

"The set's not on," Cowley told the manager in an annoyed voice.

Gadgets pushed past him and walked to the set. Nine pairs of eyes followed his every step.

"It don't matter," Gadgets grumbled. "It could still be fouling the network."

Cowley and his men watched every move Gadgets made. The manager's eyes weren't friendly either. Gadgets felt the woman was beginning to think that he didn't know what he was doing. He plunged his hand into the bag for a screwdriver. When he was sure that his hand was well hidden, he pressed the button that turned off the interference on the antenna line. He quickly unhooked the lead from the motel unit and attached it to his portable.

"Aha!" he snorted triumphantly.

"Don't I know you?" Williams asked at the same time.

While the motel manager looked at the clear picture on the portable television, Gadgets gave Williams a closer look.

"Possibly," Gadgets told the CIA agent. "You drink at the Seaman's Rest."

"I don't," Williams protested.

"Sure you do. Last time I was down there you was trying to pick up the bartender's wife."

"It wasn't me," Williams insisted.

The subject was dropped.

"Won't be a minute," Gadgets announced.

He had the back off the television before they could protest. He returned the screwdriver to his bag and palmed a small broadcasting microphone he had built from the CIA parts Lao had acquired.

He poked and prodded around the television for a moment.

"You can take it to your shop," Cowley said, his voice heavy with impatience.

The old repairman ignored him and continued to prod with a small screwdriver. Suddenly he exclaimed, "What the hell! This little bugger don't belong here."

By this time he had the full attention of everyone in the room. He pretended to remove the broadcasting microphone from the set.

"What the hell is this? Never saw anything like it." The old repairman sounded personally insulted. "It sure don't belong here."

Every CIA eye in the room was focused on the small piece of equipment in the trembling brown hand. They knew what it was.

"How the hell did he do it?" a CIA type exclaimed. "We watched this place like it was the crown jewels."

Cowley snatched the bug from the repairman and examined it to make sure it was real. Then he passed it to another man who was probably their electronics expert.

"It's made from the same type of parts that woman took from us." the man admitted.

In the meantime, the old repairman had taken a spare part from his tool bag. He installed it, attached a lead to the antenna and then reassembled the television. The angry CIA agents scarcely paid any attention to what he was doing.

Gadgets took the lead from the portable and reattached it to the television set. He then turned on the set. The picture was clear.

"That does it," Gadgets announced, closing his bag.

The CIA rushed Gadgets and the manager to the door. The agents were obviously anxious to discuss this new blunder in their security setup.

The manager was relieved that the problem had been solved and that her guests hadn't been offended. Her stern face softened.

"What do I owe you?" she asked.

"The office will send the bill," Gadgets muttered.

Without saying goodbye, he hobbled back to his truck. The bug was planted on the day he had promised.

THE ONLY ABLE TEAM warrior who wasn't exhausted from preparing for the triathlon was Lyons. The morning of the race he was up and whistling at 4:30. The others had to drag themselves out of bed.

The housekeeper didn't mind the early hour. She grinned at Lyons as she prepared his breakfast of wheat flakes, raisins and milk.

"You eat that mess and you can win anything," she told him.

Gadgets appeared next. The wrinkles had magically disappeared, but he was still dark-skinned and white-haired.

"How's Grandpa this morning?" Lyons boomed.

He was rewarded with scowls from both Gadgets and Blancanales.

Gadgets began an immediate electronic sweep of the house. Politician silently followed up with a physical search. By the time they were finished, Jane, Nikko, Mauna and Lao had joined them on the lanai. Jane and the two Hawaiians were already drinking coffee.

The rest of the team members knew that it might be a while before their next meal. Blancanales and Gadgets, surly and silent, waded into a plateful of steak and eggs. Lao tasted the wheat flakes, then she had some too, using pineapple juice instead of milk.

After the food was demolished, Politician sipped a second cup of coffee and opened the team's final discussion before the race.

"I've got a place on a press truck. If you need me, Gadgets or Lao can use a communicator."

"Mauna's going to do a run past Cowley's motel and dump the tapes. We'll listen to them as we get time," Gadgets reported. "In the meantime, I'll stick by Ironman until the transition to the cycling section is made."

Lao added, "Nikko will return the DPV when I'm through with it, then she's going to watch the rest of the race with Jane and Sherrie. Mauna will pick me up and then pick up Gadgets. We'll try to keep his Jeep somewhere close by."

"What about the shoes for the footrace?" Lyons asked, more concerned with the triathlon than security.

"Your change bags are ready," Lao told Lyons.

"Did you check them?" Gadgets asked.

"She said they were ready. She checked," Lyons said. "Do you want to be down at the beach early. It would give us a chance to see who's there and who's missing."

"Not until I've had more coffee," Gadgets grumbled. "I was up until three working on your bicycle pump."

COWLEY WAS HAVING yogurt, figs and a temper tantrum for his prerace breakfast. His small contingent of CIA operatives was gathered in his motel room, watching him eat the ugly mixture and listening to him rant.

"You found what?" Cowley demanded.

"A bug in my TV set," the electronics man muttered.

"You saw that TV repairman pull a bug out of mine. Didn't you check the rest of the sets right away?"

The victim of Cowley's interrogation nodded glumly. "I was looking for a broadcasting microphone. This one was far more sophisticated. It sent the signal up the TV antenna to a tape recorder hidden at the base of the dish. It only sends a signal when someone tells it to. Then it dumps the tapes in a few seconds."

"But you've dismantled it now?"

The CIA electronics specialist shook his head. "No, sir. I adjusted it to signal me when someone comes to dump the tape. I'm hoping to catch them at it."

Cowley chewed on a fig as he thought.

"Not bad," he conceded, "but I can think of an improvement. Who was it who told me about the Kapu'ukus?"

"I did," Williams answered. "They're a local gang with a tough reputation."

"Hire them to watch for the pickup. Tell them to rough up whoever does the dump. That way we're not involved and we don't have to admit to anyone that we're having security problems."

"Sir!" Williams protested in a shocked voice. "The Kapu'ukus are no match for Able Team. They'll all be killed."

Cowley smiled. It wasn't a pleasant smile. "All the better. We rid Hawaii of some undesirables, and Able Team gets locked up, out of our hair. I like it."

The rest of the men exchanged uneasy glances. They didn't like it, but no one was going to say so.

Williams decided to try once more. "It might not happen that way. Whoever does the dump could give the gang the slip."

"Good thought, Williams. Supply those Hawaiians with a beeper to put on the vehicle involved. Give them a finder. That way those show-offs won't be able to ditch anybody. It will teach them to plant bugs on us."

"Are you afraid Lyons will beat you?" Williams asked.

The room was hushed. The other men couldn't believe that Williams had found the nerve to speak to E-4 like that.

Cowley was now feeling more confident. He laughed. "It's close to the race. Lyons won't make the pickup. Give that gang a description of the other three members of the team. Tell them to follow whoever makes the pickup.

"I'm not worried about Lyons. He isn't trained for a race like this. He'll either be humiliated by dropping out early, or he'll kill himself. I don't care which."

"And you're willing to send these Hawaiians to their deaths?" Williams probed, sweating over his own presumption.

"Why not? We're using scum to get rid of scum," Cowley snapped.

The men looked at one another uneasily. They knew they would do what they were told.

## 17

Lyons and Gadgets arrived at the small beach an hour before the race's 7:00 A.M. start. Lyons wore only his triathlon suit and the yellow regulation bathing cap. Gadgets wore his safari suit and a small pack on his back.

The day was promising to be a hot one. The sky seemed a deeper blue than usual. The night breeze had died, and the offshore wind had not yet developed.

They stood on the edge of Kailua Pier and looked over the scene. A crowd was already gathering along the beach.

"We're not allowed to pace you," Gadgets said. "But we'll show up frequently along your route. Pol may or may not be handy on the press truck."

Lyons nodded absently. He was scanning the crowd.

"No E-4. No *spetsnaz*," he grunted.

"You better mix with the crowd," Gadgets suggested. "You're an easy target, and that funny suit you're wearing sure isn't Kevlar."

Lyons was not paying any attention. He walked toward the beach, but his eyes were on the arrival of the Russians.

The nine *spetsnaz* athletes all wore red bathing suits with the yellow swim caps. They marched toward the spot where volunteers were writing numbers on competitors' shoulders and thighs. Each athlete had to wear his number on his bare upper arms. The thigh numbering was optional, but most accepted it

Lyons pushed into the line behind the Russians, knocking an indignant, lanky female athlete out of the way. Gadgets moved in behind him.

After he was numbered, Lyons followed the *spetsnaz* onto the beach and stopped twenty feet from them. He seemed oblivious to their stares. They seemed uneasy as he methodically memorized each of their faces.

Gadgets dug a tube and a jar from his small backpack. First, he smeared sunscreen lotion over Lyons's exposed skin, then he covered him with a thick layer of Vaseline. There were many pretty volunteers who would have gladly done the job for Lyons, but he didn't want anyone to detect the flat Tekna knives that were taped to the front of his thighs.

All over the beach other participants were doing the same thing, although they limited the Vaseline to the insides of the arms and thighs—the places where swimming would produce the most friction.

Some of the athletes had taken to the water for short warm-up swims. The Russians contented themselves with a few exercises designed to stretch and loosen their muscles. Lyons just stood around, alert but physically relaxed.

Cowley's black Mercedes pulled up to the edge of the pier ten minutes before race time. The CIA information officer jumped out and joined the diminishing lineup of contestants waiting to be numbered. Two bodyguards stayed with him until he stepped onto the beach, then one applied the Vaseline while the other moved to a spot overlooking the entire beach.

As Cowley moved toward the crowd of athletes, he spotted Lyons. He left his escort and walked over to the Able Team leader.

"So you're still determined to kill yourself?" Cowley demanded.

Lyons didn't take his eyes off the Russians.

"After you," he answered.

"Not me. I have enough brains to train for these events."

"So did I. Three days."

"Three days! Idiot."

Lyons still kept his eyes on the Russians. "If they don't make their move, and I have to finish this race, I guess I'll just have to settle for second last, ahead of you."

"You wish."

Lyons didn't answer.

Cowley took the silence as a challenge. "I didn't mind helping you find equipment that would minimize the injury you'll do to yourself, but I'm serious about this race. Get in my way and I'll have you disqualified."

The CIA agent had been so intent on warning Lyons that he hadn't noticed Gadgets.

"Don't get your pecker in a knot, son," Gadgets said in his TV repairman's voice. "Just because a man's ahead of you, don't mean he's getting in your way."

Cowley glanced at Gadgets and then thrust his face within inches of the electronic genius's darkened skin. He stared at the white hair, the bleached mustache.

"Shit," Cowley said in a weak voice and walked away.

"Wonder what's wrong with him?" Gadgets mused, cracking his first smile of the day.

Excitement and anticipation increased as the triathlon's starting time drew closer. Race officials separated the onlookers from the athletes. Gadgets had to move from the immediate area.

The athletes would swim south along the coast for over a mile. Then they would round the two boats with the bright orange sails, putting the return lap a quarter of a mile farther out to sea. The swim would finish on the far side of the pier.

Gadgets would watch the swim from the pier and would then keep an eye on Ironman and the Russians through the transition to the bicycles.

The cycles were in neatly numbered slots on the pier. Volunteers would find each participant's bike as he or she emerged from the changing tents. Inside the tents other volunteers would renew the contestants' sunscreen lotion. Gadgets would stay to watch the transition, but unless trouble erupted he would keep out of the way.

The starter's pistol cracked, and thirteen hundred men and women charged into the water. Gadgets was amazed at the explosive disorder of the scene.

The sea was soon decorated by bobbing spheres of color—yellow swim caps on the men; red on the women. In the early morning sun they looked like a swarm of luminous beetles.

Small boats spotted the course, ready to offer assistance to any of the participants who needed it. Accepting their help meant instant disqualification.

When Gadgets could no longer distinguish Ironman from his competitors, he contented himself with sitting in the shade. He couldn't dispel the uneasy feeling that gripped him. There were nine *spetsnaz* in the ocean and only one Lyons.

MAUNA WHISTLED as he drove his Jeep across the island to retrieve the information gathered by Gadgets's bugs. He idolized Able Team and was proud to be part of the group around them. He had volunteered his services, but Politician had insisted that he be paid for his time and effort.

Mauna told himself that dumping the tapes involved a great deal of excitement but little danger. By the time he reached the motel, Cowley and his men would be at the race.

The Hawaiian guide parked his Jeep across from the motel. He picked up a portable cassette recorder from the seat beside him. Gadgets had gutted the inexpensive machine and had installed his own mechanics.

When Mauna Makanani pressed the red record button, the tape went into fast forward. Mauna knew that a smaller recorder located on the motel's satellite dish was furiously spinning its microcassettes, broadcasting their contents to the sophisticated receiver in his hands.

His thoughts were rudely interrupted by a voice from the sidewalk. "Hi, Mauna. How's it going?"

Mauna started, almost dropping the gizmo in his hands. "Oh! Hi, Ululani. You startled me."

"I'll say. Thought you'd go into orbit. Still worried about that haole's father?"

"Funny."

"What you got there?" Ululani asked, eyeing the whirling cassette.

"It's just a tape recorder." Mauna wondered if he'd made his voice sound too casual. "What are you doing here?" he asked, hoping to change the subject.

The thing in his hands beeped softly and stopped. The cassette was almost finished.

"The Kapu'ukus accepted a small job. I'm just here to make sure it gets done. Are you working?"

"Yeah. The guy my sister was working for had some friends come over. They hired me."

"As another guide?" The question was too sharp.

Mauna decided not to lie; it was the only way to keep the story straight.

"They don't do much sightseeing," he told Ululani. "Usually I run errands and drive them around. I've got to get back. Two of them want me to drive them to different places to watch the race."

"You'd better get going then."

Relieved, Mauna said, "You're right. See you."

He started the Jeep and pulled away from the curb, happy to leave the leader of the Sacred Fleas behind, and even happier to escape his probing questions.

Ululani watched the Jeep disappear and then walked around the bend in the road to where eight of the Kapu'ukus were waiting with motorcycles.

"Yeah," he confirmed, "it was Mauna in the Jeep. He's working for the people we want. All we have to do is follow him."

"Hey, Ululani. Do we have to use muscle on Mauna?"

The leader sighed. "Only if he interferes. Now which of you guys has that radio receiver?"

One of the members held out the black box supplied by the CIA.

"Is it getting a good signal?"

The man nodded.

"Should be. I put the magnetic transmitter on the wheel of his spare. Let's go. We've got to get this job done. We should still be able to report to the finish line in time to start giving massages."

Nine motorcycles roared to life and began to follow the Jeep on its return trip along the Hawaii Belt Road.

THE SEA HIT the Kona coast in long, smooth rollers that broke fifty feet from shore. Lyons had learned to swim along Californian beaches. It had been a while since he had been in the ocean, but he adjusted quickly. He was having no difficulty keeping E-4 and the Russians in sight.

Cowley had the long frame of a runner. Like most athletes training for the triathlon, he had maintained his swimming but had concentrated on the cycling and running because they required the most endurance. Lyons therefore found he could keep pace easily. The surprise was that the Russians weren't outstripping them. It was a surprise that left Lyons uneasy.

One Russian was swimming closely on Lyons's right. By keeping a wary eye on this competitor, the Stony Man warrior almost missed the *spetsnaz* who tried to swim up from behind. He caught the tactic just before the big swimmer overtook him. Instead of veering out of the way, Lyons kicked harder, making it difficult for the man to swim over him.

It was then that the swimmer on Lyons's left managed to push him under.

Instead of fighting it, Lyons rolled in the water and grabbed the offending arm. He tucked in his legs until he could place one foot on the *spetsnaz's* rib cage and another on his neck. A quick wrench dislocated the attacker's shoulder.

Both Lyons and the Russian came to the surface gasping for air. The other *spetsnaz* agents were now eight lengths ahead. Lyons left the disabled athlete to call for a boat and took off to catch the Russians who had now surrounded Cowley.

They were within a hundred yards of the turning point before Lyons caught up with the Russians. He decided he was better off behind them than to be surrounded by them so he held his position.

Lyons let up on his pace and contemplated the situation. His thoughts were interrupted by the appearance of three figures in scuba gear coming toward them from the depths of the sea. The small knot of athletes near Lyons made it around the boat and started back. The three divers were immediately below them, very visible in the clear water.

Two *spetsnaz* noticed Lyons and dropped back to swim on either side of him. The other six remained close to Cowley.

Cowley!

It had to be Cowley. He probably knew more about the United States's covert operations throughout the world than anyone else.

Lyons put on a burst of speed to catch up with the CIA briefing officer.

The three divers with their large swim fins shot up from below as the Russians crowded around their prize.

Everything was clear to Lyons now that he had no one to tell. The attempt to kidnap him had taken place when he was in a car identical to Cowley's.

The briefing officer was the Russian target.

Just when it seemed inevitable that the CIA man would be grabbed by the divers, a streak of yellow and blue moved between the three men and their target. Lyons's attempt to overtake Cowley to warn him was thwarted when the Russian swimmers pacing the blond warrior grabbed both of his arms.

## 18

Lao Ti used the diver propulsion vehicle to pace the competitors from her position a half mile offshore. She stayed about fifty feet below the swimmers. At that depth, keeping track of Lyons's bright green suit was difficult, but not impossible. Lao's own blue outfit combined with the gray of the DPV to keep her from being spotted.

The vehicle somewhat resembled a snowmobile. It was propelled by a small electric motor. The batteries accounted for a great deal of the weight of the machine. It carried two hundred cubic feet of air for its divers, which added another seventy pounds to its overall weight. On land the DPV was too heavy to manage comfortably. In the water it had neutral buoyancy—no weight at all.

It would easily allow one diver to pace the swimmers, and it had just enough range to pull someone for the entire race.

Lao could have used fins to keep up, but she couldn't have carried a sufficient air supply while she used that much energy. However, she did have the two small European tanks on her back and could easily switch from the sled's regulator to her own air supply. The mouthpiece trailed from her shoulder.

Lao also spotted the three divers swimming in from the open ocean. They carried eighty-cubic-foot tanks to extend their range. She couldn't be sure that they were a menace, but she began to move in.

When she was closer, she saw that two of the men had octopus rigs on their regulators, rigs that allowed a second mouthpiece to share one air supply. Divers often did this as a safety precaution on difficult dives. The rig would also be useful in an underwater kidnapping.

She switched to her own air supply as she steered to intercept the underwater menace. Two of the scuba divers turned to meet her as the third streaked toward the surface.

Lao rammed the sled into one diver. It wasn't going fast enough to do more than keep him out of her way. She pushed off from the vehicle and rose behind the diver who was making for the surface. The sled stopped when her hand was removed from the drive button.

As she stretched for the man above and ahead of her, Lao managed to slip off both of the swim fins. Before her target could react, she was over him and yanking the mouthpiece from his mouth. She then pushed herself away from the diver just as one of his colleagues grabbed for her.

Lao Ti eluded that diver's grasp by catching his hands and applying pressure to his wrists. He tried unsuccessfully to kick loose.

The Able Team warrior let go of the man's hands and grabbed his diving mask. She placed her feet on his chest and pushed herself away, pulling the mask off his face. The man blinked several times as he tried to adjust his eyes to the salt water.

Moments are precious when fighting for life.

Lao Ti turned to face the man she had rammed with the DPV. He had drawn his diving knife. The small woman drew one of the flat knives she had purchased. It was razor sharp, and its size offered minimum resistance in the water in comparison to her opponent's larger knife.

The Russian fighter lunged and thrust his knife. Lao's left arm moved quickly through the water to deflect the weapon. Her right hand flashed down, slicing the inside of the wrist of his knife hand. The sight of his blood spurting out to cloud the water distracted the knife fighter. It was a fatal distraction.

Lao kicked to one side, leaving her victim to grasp at his cut wrist. Lao's knife flashed again, severing his air hose.

The man with the one flipper managed to grab her from behind, but it took his two hands to get a good grip on the small, wiry form. He couldn't get to her air supply, but the knife-wielding diver without the mask was closing in.

Lao simply brought the small blade down, sinking it into a thigh behind her. Then she raised her arms and tried to force herself from the Russian's hold. Fighting for a better grip, he wrapped his arms around her neck.

Lao doubled her leg and drove it into the face mask of the approaching diver. The force of the kick propelled him backward and dislodged both mask and mouthpiece. His wild swipe with the knife was countered by her other foot, which kicked his arm up to cut water over Lao's head.

As he fought to clear and replace his mouthpiece, Lao reached up and grabbed one of the arms crushing her neck. Her strong fingers dug into the elbow and pressed it up. Her other hand seized the wrist, bent it and forced it down. It was a standard lifesaving technique that Lao had often used in tense situations.

The leverage was applied body-to-body. There was no way to resist. Suddenly the attacker found himself held in a hammerlock, with one small hand on his elbow and Lao's other hand forcing his own arm back and up between his shoulder blades. There wasn't enough leverage to dislocate the shoulder.

Lao's hand slipped from the wrist to the top of his tank. Four quick turns and the air supply was off. The diver momentarily forgot Lao as he struggled to reach his own tanks.

She turned her attention to the third man, who now had his mouthpiece in place. Lao swam toward him as the wounded diver behind her fought to reach the surface. The two adversaries swam in a tighter and tighter circle until it was impossible to determine who was the hunted and who was the hunter.

Lao powered herself ahead with two fast strokes. She grabbed the diver's swim fin straps behind the ankles and yanked both flippers off. Then she turned and kicked away, leaving him behind. The racers had passed by overhead. Without fins, the Russian could no longer catch up to his target.

Lao Ti found the rented DPV and switched to its air supply. She steered for the sheltered cove where the DPV's trailer was hidden.

Both Mauna and Nikko Makanani were waiting for her. The three of them wrestled the DPV onto the trailer.

"I'll return this and then check in on the race at a point close to the airport," Nikko said. "Later, I'll join the princess. She has a table on the second floor of a restaurant near the finish line. The race passes there several times. Mauna knows where to find me if you want anything."

Lao smiled her thanks and stripped off the blue diving suit. She didn't bother to towel off but pulled on jeans and a light shirt. She also put on socks and a pair of hiking boots. She knew that sandals wouldn't be effective on the loose rock that made up so much of the island's terrain.

Then Lao Ti climbed into the Jeep beside Mauna, and he started for the pier. She immediately picked up the doctored tape recorder, plugged a small earphone into one ear and began monitoring the material that Mauna had recorded from the surveillance device at Cowley's motel.

Lao was too intent to notice the roar of motorcycles from somewhere behind them.

THE TWO SPETSNAZ ATHLETES QUICKLY REALIZED that they had taken on more trouble than they had expected when they grabbed Lyons by the arms.

The blond warrior forced his arms down and pushed his head out of the water so that he could take in a lungful of air. The attackers hadn't calculated on Lyons's greasy body. Their grips slipped. Lyons pushed his foot into one attacker's stomach and easily pulled his right arm free.

Before the Russian could recover, the Able Team warrior's free hand swung to the leg of his suit. He yanked loose the Tekna knife he had taped to his left thigh. Ignoring the grappling hands that were trying to find a new grip, Lyons swung the knife into the abdomen of the *spetsnaz* who was still hanging onto his left arm. The killer let go of Lyons to hold himself instead.

The grappler no longer wanted anything to do with Lyons. He turned and stroked hard to catch up with the rest of his team.

The surviving Russians were frustratingly pacing E-4. It was too late to try another kidnapping in the sea. They would have to stay with him and try again during the cycling part of the race.

Lyons let go of the knife and concentrated on the swim. His main objective was to emerge from the water in time to warn Cowley that he was the target of the *spetsnaz* plot. The encounters with the Russian assassins had diverted Lyons. He was now two hundred yards behind the CIA officer.

Lyons made it around the pier and out of the water just as the briefing officer and the Russian athletes were being handed their bicycles by eager volunteers. He noticed that Gadgets stood just behind the line of police holding the crowd back, but he knew he would only lose precious time by trying to talk to him. Lyons wanted to catch up to Cowley as quickly as possible.

The Able Team warrior had to go to the change tent even though he wasn't changing clothes. When he got there, he was handed his transition bag. Lyons allowed a volunteer to smear him with more sunscreen, but he didn't waste time toweling off.

He slipped on the cycling shoes and helmet and then yanked on the mesh jacket that had his race number on the back and a large pocket for supplies. Lyons quickly filled the pocket with fresh figs and invert-sugar candy. When he emerged from the tent, almost two minutes later, a volunteer was already wheeling up his bike.

Lyons took time to grab a banana from a table. He quickly peeled it and stuffed the entire thing into his mouth.

When his bicycle arrived, he grunted his thanks, jumped on and started to pedal. Once he was going, he coasted while he slid his shoes into the toe clips. He headed up Palani Road toward Queen Kaahumanu Highway. Lyons was in the last third of the pack. Cowley, surrounded by Russians, was somewhere in the middle of the group. Lyons concentrated on pushing pedals.

Lyons had known that Gadgets would reposition himself so that they could exchange a few words before the Ironman started cycling. But with a banana crammed into his mouth, Lyons had motioned for Gadgets to meet him at the next contact point. By then he would have warned Cowley and could take the time to pass on the message to the rest of Able Team.

The competitors were already jockeying for position; they were looking for a comfortable slot where each could establish his own pace. The first part of the course was predominantly uphill, and Lyons quickly appreciated the low range of the bike's gears. He pushed steadily, sipping frequently from the plastic bottle filled with Gatorade that he kept in the bike's clip.

At the aid station on Palani Road, Lyons exchanged the nearly empty bottle for a fresh one with his number on it. He grabbed three more bananas from a table and pushed off.

A flatbed truck, crowded with news photographers, had just passed the first aid station. Blancanales was making notes from his position in one corner of the truck.

"Got any comments to make so far?" he called to Lyons.

"I hope to catch up with the big talker," Lyons said.

"He's two minutes ahead," Blancanales returned in a soft voice.

"He's the target."

Rosario Blancanales let out a low whistle and nodded to indicate that he would pass the information on.

Lyons applied himself to the pedals once again. He didn't catch sight of Cowley or the Russians until he turned onto the highway.

They were cresting a slight rise about half a mile ahead. Lyons knew he wasn't pacing himself properly. But he wasn't there to finish the race; he was there to thwart the Russians. Cowley would be the intelligence prize of the century if they managed the snatch.

The wind was rising steadily, and already the cyclists were having difficulty holding a straight line. Lyons grimly continued to push the pedals, slowly passing one competitor after another. It was a grim race, and the sweat was pouring down his face, though it was dried by the wind before it could drip from his chin.

The Russians were concentrating on keeping up with Cowley. They weren't aware of Ironman's approach until he was ten feet behind the trailing Russian. The man looked over his shoulder and then quickly poured on the speed. He overtook the other *spetsnaz* and spread the word that trouble was on their tail once more. Several glanced back anxiously.

Lyons ignored them and continued to pedal strongly. The Russians obviously felt that having him in their midst was a safety precaution, so they let him by without any trouble. He was gaining on Cowley, who had been pacing himself for the entire race and not just for the one sprint. When he pulled alongside, the CIA agent looked startled.

"You still with us?"

Lyons didn't bother to answer the obvious. It was getting more difficult to hold the road as the wind rose. He couldn't miss this chance to brief the CIA agent.

"It's you they plan to snatch," Lyons growled at Cowley.

"What are you talking about?"

"Why do you think the Russians have you surrounded? You're the target."

"They're just athletes."

"So are you, and they're inviting you to Russia."

Cowley looked around and then shrugged. They veered to avoid a press photographer who had stepped onto the road.

"You're nuts! There's too much press coverage. Stop trying to scare me out of the race."

Having expended that much energy, Cowley applied himself to outdistancing Lyons and his bothersome talk.

Angrily Lyons strained to keep up.

"Think about it while you can," he shouted at Cowley.

Cowley steadily increased his speed. The Russians had no choice but to pump along with their target. They had to try to keep him surrounded until they could attempt another snatch. Cowley's action left Lyons no latitude either. He followed along, trying to catch his wind, and hoping that he would have some energy left when the Russians made their move.

Cowley glanced over his shoulder. Lyons was behind him by seven bike lengths and grimly hanging on. If Cowley went any faster, he would burn the reserves of energy he would need to finish the race. He had trained for three years for the Hawaiian Ironman. Other triathlons were tough, but this was the real one. His reputation as a serious contender in the triathlon world was at stake. He had to finish the Ironman.

They passed another aid station. Determined to outdistance Lyons, Cowley didn't slow down. He merely accepted a wet sponge that was tossed to him by a volunteer. The Russians didn't stop either, and they ignored the sponges. Lyons paused long enough to grab another couple of bananas. There was no bottle for him here. He had thought it would be enough to leave one at every second station.

Lyons's pause was brief, but it was enough to put the Russians and their prey a quarter of a mile ahead of him. It was at this point that Lyons realized he had squandered his energy foolishly.

He had been so intent on warning Cowley that he had used energy he should have been conserving. A moment's reflection would have told him that E-4 wasn't about to quit the race.

Lyons settled down to a steady pace. He kept the Russians in sight, but didn't try to close the gap between them. He would be safer with the seven surviving Russian athletes ahead of him where he could see them.

But he hadn't seen the rest of the Russian group—the killers and terrorists who posed as coaches, masseurs and water boys. They were strangely absent from the scene, and the thought made the Ironman uneasy.

He glanced around at the barren landscape with its parched vegetation. There was no sign of Gadgets or Lao or of the press truck Blancanales was using. Although the race was a media event and much of the course was crawling with photographers and television crews, there were stretches the media found void of interest, stretches without spectators or witnesses. It wouldn't be easy, but the *spetsnaz* could use such an area to abduct Cowley.

Lyons still didn't try to close the gap. If they stopped Cowley, he would reach them before they could do much. But he would need help, and there was still no sign of the rest of the team.

Lyons was beginning to understand why most cyclists wore heavy gloves. Bent over the bicycle and pushing hard, he had to pull down against the handgrips to keep the high pressure on the pedals. His hands were beginning to blister.

The farther north they went, the stronger the wind became. Race officials patrolled the blacktop, watching for infractions of the drafting rules. A racer who ignored the distance requirement between cyclists, and who used another competitor to break the force of the wind, was instantly disqualified.

Many of the bicycles were wobbling, and everyone was gearing down. Even the scooters and small motorcycles being used by officials were having trouble as the wind increased.

Blancanales's press truck passed on its way to take a new position. The cameramen had given up trying to grab shots against the wind and motion of the truck.

Ironman put on a burst of speed to get Blancanales's attention.

"Watch E-4," he shouted.

Politician nodded. Several newsmen thought they were getting a tip on an athlete who would make a sudden break to lead the pack. They flipped through their programs, looking for the number of a competitor named "Effor."

Lyons watched as the truck passed Cowley and the Russians. A couple of the cameramen struggled to get some footage of the Russians, but Lyons knew that not much of the tape would be usable because of the wind and motion of the truck. Soon the truck moved on.

Lyons's bottle was empty. He had exchanged it at the last aid station, which meant he had well over five miles to go before he could get a refill. He settled down to make the distance go as quickly as possible.

To his surprise, Lyons found himself gaining on E-4 and the Russians. He concentrated on the distance over the next three minutes until he realized that the Russians had bunched up ahead of Cowley and were slowing him down. Another small pack of cyclists was grouped up ahead of the Russians. Apparently Mother Russia's finest didn't want Cowley to overtake the other cyclists. Lyons was sure it meant they intended to make their move soon.

Ironman slowed down at the next aid stand for more Gatorade and two bananas. The winds were getting stronger. One competitor—a woman who looked fit and in her twenties—suddenly collapsed on the road. Paramedics and volunteers rushed to help her, drawing the judges' attention from the Russians' attempt to block Cowley.

Ironman started after them once more. His shoulders and back ached, but he ignored the pain. He had to catch up with Cowley before it was too late. If only he knew where Gadgets and Lao were.

It didn't take Lyons long to overtake Cowley, who was weaving back and forth in angry frustration. The Russians would box him tightly and slow him down. Then if the lead or tail man signaled the approach of the press or a race official, the Russians would spurt ahead, leaving a legal distance between themselves and the CIA agent.

Lyons timed his play for the next interruption. When the Russians spread out, he strained against the pedals and handlebars in an effort to overtake Cowley. The CIA man glanced over to see who was passing him. When he saw Lyons, the briefing officer shouted at him against the wind.

"You put them up to this. You're having them slow me down so you can beat me."

The charge was so outrageous that Lyons thought the Bostonian had just made the first joke in his life. But the Able Team warrior had no time to laugh.

"They'll make their move in the next few minutes," he shouted.

"What move?"

Lyons wasn't sure, but he knew it had to be now.

The group was within eight miles of the turnaround point at Hawi. The lava moonscape had yielded to the lush, vividly green tropical vegetation. Roaring winds off the ocean whipped at grasses, ferns and palms until the road was bordered by a blur of motion.

Like an apparition, a lone spectator appeared in the middle of the deserted highway.

Two Russian cyclists each grabbed something from the figure and then wheeled in to bracket Lyons and Cowley. Each *spetsnaz* steadied his racing bike with one hand and, with the other, pointed a Llama Small Frame .32 at the Americans.

## 19

Gadgets's forehead was lined with worry by the time he met Lao and Mauna.

"Ironman wanted to tell me something, but he was in one hell of a rush. I couldn't get close, but something's up," he told Lao.

She didn't question him. Blancanales and Schwarz had worked with Lyons for so long that they seemed to know what he was thinking. It was such a close relationship that she often felt like an outsider. So she nodded once to indicate that she understood Gadgets's concern, then put the earphone back in her ear and continued to listen to the material picked up by Gadgets's bugs.

"Get in," Mauna said. "We'll get ahead of him, and you can ask him then."

Gadgets made no move to get into the Jeep. Instead he unslung his pack and opened it.

"Did you empty the dump?" he asked Mauna.

"Guess so. The tape stopped moving, and the machine beeped."

"Any trouble?"

"I'm not sure."

Gadgets practically jumped into the Jeep. "What do you mean you're not sure?"

"While I was waiting for the tape to stop, a guy named Ululani came over and asked me some questions. But I didn't see any other members of the Kapu'ukus, and he let me go. So I guess he was just being friendly.''

"The Kapu who?"

"The Kapu'ukus are a local club. They enter the canoe races, but they're also a motorcycle gang. They have a tough reputation, but they're the ones who helped me get away from the Russians."

Mauna had to turn his head while he talked because Gadgets was on the move. He had pulled another of his homemade gizmos from his pack and was sweeping the Jeep for bugs. When he reached the back of the Jeep, the sound emitted by the sweeper increased in both pitch and volume. Gadgets turned it off and vaulted into the Jeep.

"Find a nice deserted spot for a business meeting," he told Mauna. "Your friend put an electronic tracer on your spare tire."

Mauna let out the clutch and started inland.

"Where is it?" he asked.

"I left it where it was. If someone's watching, I don't want him to know I've found anything."

"I don't believe this. I just don't believe it."

Neither Gadgets nor Lao tried to deal with his disbelief.

Mauna found a deserted piece of lava flow east of town. Gadgets had him park the Jeep off the road but in plain sight. Then the three moved into the low vegetation to wait. Lao took the tape with her and continued to listen.

Three minutes later nine motorcycles roared by. They stopped another hundred yards along the road. Their drivers dismounted and stood looking back at the Jeep.

"That's the Kapu'ukus," Mauna said to Gadgets.

"Hush," Gadgets answered.

After five minutes of indecision, the motorcyclists got back on their machines and drove over to the empty Jeep. Gadgets and Lao rose out of the underbrush and moved in on the gang from opposite directions. The gang members were too preoccupied with the empty Jeep to notice the new arrivals until the two Able Team members were within six feet of the group.

When the members realized they had been caught, they turned off their motors and dismounted. They looked around, expecting to see a much larger force than a white-haired man and a small oriental woman.

Mauna could contain himself no longer. He ran toward them, waving his arms.

"Take it easy on them," he yelled. "They don't work for the Russians."

Ululani looked at Mauna and grinned as he asked, "Worried about your employers' health?"

Mauna was frantic. "No, just get out. Those two will kill you!"

A gang member who was almost as large as the leader but wider across the shoulders laughed. He grabbed Lao by the upper arms in an effort to lift her off her feet.

Lao swung her arms up over her head, breaking the hold. Her cupped hands swung to the Hawaiian's ears. The action sent a jolt of compressed air to the eardrums. Though Lao avoided using enough force to rupture the eardrums, the compressive force was like a firecracker exploding in each ear. The gang member forgot Lao and sank to his knees with his hands over his ears.

Deciding that the fight had started, three gang members charged Gadgets. They ignored Mauna's warning. The three men thought it would be fun to push the old man back and forth between them.

Gadgets understood that these young men hadn't been hired by the Russians. They had trailed Mauna from the Puopelu Ranch Motel and therefore had probably been sent by Cowley. But they were strong, and there were eight of them. Gadgets decided that as long as no weapons were produced he would do his best to keep the Kapu'ukus in one piece

While he was making that decision, he had been pushed back and forth twice. He staggered around, waiting to see if any more gang members would join the game.

Ululani and two of his lieutenants went to the aid of Lao's victim. Two more joined the circle to play push-the-old-man. Gadgets decided he had as many in the game as he was going to attract.

When a hand shoved him from behind, he staggered forward as if off-balance. The man ahead put out two hands to keep Gadgets upright before sending him staggering back. Gadgets moved under the outstretched arms and sank his fist into the man's solar plexus. Then he whirled and caught the next man in the shin.

Gadgets ran two steps across the circle, sprang into the air, tucked and released both feet into the face of another gang member. Then he landed on his feet and spun to attack a fourth member of the circle.

This one had seen enough. He let his knees buckle and collapsed under the Stony Man warrior's blow. As Gadgets's momentum carried him over the prone form, the man wrapped his arms around Gadgets's legs and brought him down. The fifth member of the circle and the one who had had his shin kicked jumped on top of the downed form.

Lao Ti stood waiting for Ululani and his two friends to close in, then she worked the inside of the circle in classical *aikido* style. She grabbed the first wrist that was thrust her way and redirected its momentum. The Able Team warrior swung the gang member like a weight on a string, using him to bowl over another attacker.

She used the counterforce to spin herself into Ululani. He tried to encircle her with his arms, but she drove her elbow into his stomach.

As he collapsed, she told him calmly, "I could have connected three inches higher and killed you."

At the moment Ululani wasn't sure that killing him wouldn't have been the kinder alternative. As he fought to breathe, he realized that Mauna had meant his warning.

One of the other gang members was getting back to his feet. Lao casually kicked him in the face and knocked him onto his back.

Mauna couldn't explain what he did next. For the first part of the fight he had stood in undecided agony. He didn't want to see any of the Kapu'ukus get hurt; they had befriended him. On the other hand, he couldn't stand by and watch the two haoles beaten. They had saved him from the Russians and had treated him well.

When Gadgets went down, Mauna's decision was made by his body, not his mind. He leaped on top of the heap and started to pull the Sacred Fleas off Gadgets's hide.

Gadgets was far from helpless at the bottom of the pile. As he had fallen, he had twisted so that he would land on his back. Now he brought his legs up. When the weight of one man was removed, he straightened his legs and sent the other one flying. A third charged in only to get kicked on the thigh and lose his balance.

"Hold it," Ululani shouted. "Everyone back off."

The Kapu'ukus were only too happy to obey the command.

Ululani turned to Lao. "You're armed. I felt the weapon before you did me in with your elbow."

She nodded.

"Why didn't you use it?"

Lao went back to where she had been hiding before the ambush and retrieved the souped-up tape recorder. She put the earphone in her ear and hit the rewind button. Everyone watched in silence as she found the place on the tape she wanted.

'Listen to this,'' she commanded Ululani, handing him the earphone.

The first thing the club leader heard was Williams's voice saying, "Sir! The Kapu'ukus are no match for Able Team. They'll get killed."

When Ululani heard the answer, he pulled the earphone from his ear and swore long and loudly.

"We been sucked," he told the others. "That bastard thought he'd get us killed."

When Mauna saw that the crisis was over, he let out a loud sigh. It brought smiles to several faces.

"Are you guys still going to be able to massage?" he asked. He turned and explained to Gadgets and Lao. "The Ironman's a big thing on the island. Almost everyone helps out one way or another. The athletes are in rough shape by the time they finish the race, so each is guaranteed a massage. The Kapu'ukus are the best masseurs on the island."

Lao and Gadgets exchanged glances. They were interested in these tough young men who raced their war canoe, hired their muscle and then volunteered to massage athletes.

Ululani was taking stock of his men. "We're okay. At least we will be by the time we report to the massage tent. But I'm not sure if Joe and Mike can ride their bikes back."

Gadgets looked at the motorcycles. "How about if Mauna drives your men back and you loan us the two cycles. We'll return them to the massage tent after the race."

"You'd do that?"

"Anything for a friend."

"You can trust them," Mauna told the Kapu'ukus.

Gadgets and the leader shook hands. Ululani strode over to Lao who was still brushing her jeans off. "I'd fall in love with you, but I don't think it would be safe to have a woman who could beat me up," he told her.

A laughing Lao and Gadgets chose the two cycles they wanted and took off. They had been away from Lyons far too long, and with the *spetsnaz* around a man could need his friends—suddenly.

WHEN CARL LYONS SAW the weapons, his battle instincts took over. He reacted so quickly that the Russians didn't know if he had even seen their guns.

Ironman shouted "Go!" at Cowley and steered his cycle into the *spetsnaz* on his right. The Russians were tightly packed around their targets. The swerve caused an accident that dumped four of the seven Russian cyclists.

Cowley, not wanting to be delayed by an inquiry into the accident, raced away. He was unaware that there were weapons trained on him. But a dead CIA agent was of little use to the Russians. The three who were still on bikes had no choice but to tuck their guns away and take off after the CIA briefing officer. They would stay with him until there were no witnesses and try again to capture him.

The four grounded Russians rolled clear of their bicycles. Lyons pushed himself straight back, pulling his toes from the clips. He straddled his cycle, standing over the rear wheel. With an angry burst of Russian, one *spetsnaz* agent kicked the spokes in Lyons's front wheel.

Lyons ignored the childish gesture. He was too busy removing the air pump from the bike frame.

One tall Russian raised his Llama and looked around. There would be no witnesses. He could kill this interfering bastard and be on his way before anyone knew what was happening.

But the lanky *spetsnaz* waited too long before making his kill decision. Lyons had the pump free, and he lunged with it like a fencer. The end of the pump jammed into the gunman's chest, and there was a muffled gunshot.

Gadgets had transformed Ironman's bicycle pump into a disguised bang stick, a shark-killing device that fires a bullet when the tip connects with the carnivore's hide. This particular shark dropped his automatic and folded. He had muffed his last hand.

Two more *spetsnaz* regained their feet, fumbling for weapons. Lyons's long leg caught one on the side of the head, sending him sprawling on top of the fourth killer.

The sound of motorcycles filled the air.

Lyons still had the bang stick in his hand. It wouldn't fire again until it was reloaded, but it made a good weapon. Lyons slammed it into the side of another Russian's head. The man dropped to the ground and lost consciousness.

Lyons jumped onto the back of one of the two men who were struggling to get up.

Gadgets and Lao chose that moment to drive up on their borrowed motorcycles. More triathlon competitors appeared over the brow of a hill. The three surviving Russians didn't immediately associate the white-haired man and skinny woman with their enemy. They quickly became more concerned about covering up the incident than they were about killing Lyons.

Two of them bent over their dead comrade. The third covered Lyons with his Llama Small Frame.

"Is all right," one said in heavily accented English to the gathering crowd. "Heatstroke. Is all right."

The passing racers were curious, but couldn't take the time to stop. Every bit of strength and concentration that they had went into keeping their bikes upright and moving forward. Each competitor had only one concern: beat the *mumuku* winds that rushed inland from the Pacific; beat the *mumuku* and be a finisher in the Ironman. Race officials would be along soon to care for the fallen.

Lyons paid no attention to the weapon pointed at him. Gadgets and Lao had instinctively stopped in positions outflanking the enemy. As Lyons filled in his teammates, he picked up a damaged Russian cycle and undid the wing nuts on the front wheel. He substituted the Russian wheel for his broken front one.

"If I can't repair the cycle, I'm out of the race. Cowley's ahead. He's the target. They tried to kidnap him once in the water and again here. Keep an eye on him. You can't stay too close or he'll be disqualified. I'll try to catch up and hang in a while longer."

While Lyons issued orders, Gadgets reloaded the bang stick and returned it to Ironman's bike frame. He then stepped away and unobtrusively covered the Russians. They were making no moves while other competitors were in sight.

Less than a minute later Lyons said, "Ready."

Lao and Gadgets wheeled away to try to find and protect Cowley before another snatch was attempted.

Lyons glanced at the Russians. The *spetsnaz* were too busy to clash with the Able Team leader at the moment. Anxious to prevent an inquiry before their teammates had another chance to snatch Cowley, they were dragging the body out of sight. Even the man with the gun was helping. Lyons also knew they only had a jumble of parts with which to fix their bikes.

Shrugging his shoulders, Lyons left them. He was anxious to catch up with Cowley and to get him out of the race to somewhere he could be protected.

It was Lyons's intention to pedal only until he caught up to Cowley, who by this time should be doubling back for the return leg. However, the track made a lengthy loop at the turnaround, and Lyons missed his objective. He found himself pedaling south again as fast as he had pumped north.

He passed cyclists who were forced to walk their bikes through the body-bending winds.

Lyons's aches had grown to a point where he couldn't tell one from another. His body was simply a generalized field of pain. His breathing was labored, and he was sweating profusely. He realized he wasn't replacing moisture nearly as quickly as he was using it. He took another long drink of Gatorade.

On the return trip the wind was mostly at his back. The sun was just past the meridian and was beating down on him. It was easier to pump with the wind behind him, but it was a lot hotter. He paused at an aid station to grab wet sponges and take on plain water.

The bicycle wobbled even more when he started out again. He pushed south steadily, wringing sponges over his head and soaking the handkerchief that draped his neck.

There was no sign of the rest of Able Team so there was no way to catch up to Cowley any faster. Lyons wasn't even sure what would happen if the Russians made another attempt to snatch the briefing officer. Would any of Able Team arrive on time? Or could the U.S.S.R. dogs snatch Cowley and disappear before Lyons showed?

The idea of going through the rest of the race trying to catch up made Lyons shudder. Normally he would be enjoying this. But he had already spent too much energy. He had no intention of finishing the grueling triathlon. For the first time it occurred to Lyons that Cowley might be right. It was possible the Stony Man warrior would kill himself from heat and exertion—if the *spetsnaz* didn't get him first.

Lyons pumped the pedals steadily, monotonously, ignoring his pain. He scarcely noticed the dozens of dropouts who were now walking along the highway, pushing their expensive bikes or simply resting at the roadside, kneading exhausted muscles. Although his body cried out for more energy, he was too hot to eat, too exhausted to care that his palms were heavily blistered. He wanted only to catch up to

Cowley once more. He had to remove the idiot from the race. By force if necessary.

He changed his empty bottle for a full one and grabbed a handful of orange sections at the next aid station. A volunteer applied more sunscreen to his exposed skin. He was already getting slightly red because the perspiration was washing away some of the lotion. The big warrior was aware of none of this.

Lyons's mind was recording the events without being aware of them. There was too much pain to allow immediate awareness. His battle conditioning and strong survival instinct kept him moving, kept him pushing on those hated pedals.

Another hour and a half passed in a blur. Lyons finally caught sight of Cowley far ahead of him and cycling past a cluster of tourist hotels. They were still north of the airport; there was another thirty miles to go to finish the bike race's 112-mile course.

It took another ten minutes of grim pedaling to close the distance. Lyons's fog cleared long enough for him to admit to a grudging admiration for Cowley. The man had to be a superbly conditioned athlete to last this long under these conditions. He showed no signs of exhaustion. Lyons was beginning to see spots in front of his eyes.

Dimly he heard the roar of a motorcycle and somehow knew that Gadgets and Lao Ti had found some way to move with the race and keep Cowley in sight. When he got closer, he saw how, but he was too foggy to appreciate the ingenuity of it.

Somehow Gadgets had acquired a professional movie camera. Lao drove the cycle while Gadgets sat with his back to hers and pretended to film Cowley. Their presence seemed to have discouraged the *spetsnaz*. There was no sign of them.

Lao dropped back until they were just ahead of Lyons. Gadgets pretended to be getting a close-up of Lyons's pain-racked features. Lao watched for race officials. There would be questions asked if someone realized they were letting Lyons coast with them.

"Where's the other motorcycle?" Lyons puffed.

"We used it for a deposit on the camera. I wanted to capture your dying gasps for future generations of Americans."

Lao gunned the cycle and took them ahead ten yards to Cowley. Lyons had had enough of a break from coasting with the motorcycle so that he was able to catch up as well.

"Thanks," Cowley puffed when he saw Lyons. "Those Russians were up to something, but you scared them off."

"Not for long. Quit. While you can." Talking took a lot out of Lyons. His lungs were pumping to full capacity. He had little breath left for chatter.

"Why are you trying to get me to quit? Neither of us will win this race."

Lyons didn't answer for a while. His legs were telling him they were tired of cycling. They wanted to be walking, or maybe staggering, but definitely not steadily pushing a bicycle.

Lyons and Cowley passed a tourist strip crowded with shoulder-to-shoulder resorts and hotels. The road was lined with spectators who were straining to identify the cyclists as they raced past.

To the athletes, the scene was a blur of hot colors, a blend of bikinis, Hawaiian shirts and muumuus. A steady chant of "Go! Go! Go!" rose from the crowd and hung suspended in the heat. Behind the words floated a haze of metallic sound. Excited spectators rattled pebbles in beer cans to cheer their favorites.

From this point only twenty-six miles remained in the cycling course.

The bicycles would be dropped farther down the coast at a swank resort south of Kona, where agony event number three would begin.

The last event was a 26.2-mile marathon back along Alii Drive, through Kona and along the scorching highway to a point some six miles north of the town. Turning south again, those still able to run, walk or crawl would reenter Kona for the fourth time that day to cross the finish line at the pier where the swim and bicycle events had started that morning.

Nikko's voice suddenly shouted from the crowd, so shrilly it could be heard clearly over the general clamor, "It's Lono! He's still in the race."

The Hawaiians looked at the heavily muscled cyclist with the blond hair flapping through the openings in his helmet. He was the one wearing the ridiculously mixed colors. Nikko's comment excited their imaginations, and perhaps their sense of humor. Whatever the reason, people started to chant.

"Lono, Lono, Lono." The chant was picked up by hundreds of spectators. Many didn't even know what the name signified.

"Lono, Lono, Lono." The chant built. It sped ahead of the racers.

Lyons shouted to Gadgets, "Find the Russians and watch them. I'll keep an eye on E-4."

Gadgets said something to Lao Ti, and she slowed the cycle, turning to the north. Lyons steeled himself for the task of staying in the race for a little longer, just until he could get Blancanales to cover Cowley.

"I've had enough of your attempts to get me out of the race," Cowley shouted. "I'm losing you now."

The CIA agent suddenly strained against the handlebars and applied himself to the pedals. His sleek bicycle began to slowly pull away from Lyons.

**20**

When Lyons told Lao Ti and Gadgets to find the remaining *spetsnaz* athletes, Lao turned the motorcycle and headed back to the scene of the most recent skirmish with them. It was a slim chance, but someone might have seen them leaving the area.

Lao had to stop while Gadgets turned to face the front of the cycle. Their cover as news photographer and assistant had not yet been questioned, but it would be if Gadgets was sitting so the only pictures he could possibly take were the cyclists' backs. They moved against the flow of the racers on the opposite side of the road. Gadgets looked through the viewfinder as if searching for just the right shot.

Lao drove as fast as their cover permitted back to the spot south of Hawi where the *spetsnaz* had made the mistake of pulling their handguns. There were no police officers, and there wasn't a body. The Russians had obviously succeeded in hiding their dead companion. They seemed to have vanished along with the body.

"We've got the right place," Gadgets said, indicating a pile of broken racing bicycles in the ditch. "But where did they go from here?"

Lao stopped the motorcycle, and Gadgets swung off the seat to look around. A cycling shoe caught his eye. It was on a piece of bare rock forty feet from the road toward the ocean. Lao put down the kickstand, and they went to the shoe to investigate.

The shoe itself offered no clue, but they decided to push on toward the beach. The ground was getting rougher and was covered with thick bush and low plants that made the walking difficult.

When they reached a patch of broken shrubbery, they spotted the body. It had been dropped only a hundred feet from the ocean. The two warriors stopped and looked at each other.

Gadgets spoke the question that was on both of their minds, "Why take it this far and just leave it?"

Lao Ti answered by making a headfirst dive into a shallow depression. Gadgets did a shoulder roll and then followed her. He didn't want to waste any time asking her what she was doing. Automatic pistol fire followed him all the way, snapping over his head in angry frustration.

"Got my answer," Gadgets muttered. "They wanted to lure us here. That's why the shoe was so obvious."

Lao produced a MAC-11 from a leg clip. Gadgets pulled his Big Mack from under a loose shirt. But there wasn't much they could do with either of them. The depression was shallow. If they popped up to shoot, their heads would be blown off long before they zeroed in on a target.

Lao worked a fist-sized piece of rock loose from the thin soil and heaved it  No one shot at the rock, but two bullets passed within inches of her wrist when she threw it. She looked at Gadgets.

He shrugged, indicating that he had no more ideas than she did.

She tossed a smaller rock but was careful to keep her arm lower. One Russian tried to shoot her hand. The rest held their fire.

Then something rustled in the grass at the lip of the depression. Gadgets automatically fired a three-shot burst. It didn't stop the rock from rolling a few more feet before coming to a stop.

Lao realized she had started something she couldn't stop. It was easy for the Russians to toss rocks at them; it was difficult to toss them back without being shot at. The Russians had a target; Lao Ti didn't.

"Most of the rocks are coming from that direction," Gadgets grunted, pointing with his subgun.

Lao brushed aside a rock the size of both her fists and nodded.

"On the count of three?"

She nodded again. The rocks were coming faster and more accurately.

"One, two, three," Gadgets droned.

They both popped up and sent raking autofire back along the trajectory of most of the rocks, then dropped down again just as angry death hornets buzzed and snapped over their heads.

"Hah," Gadgets muttered. "They were so busy tossing rocks they forgot to keep us covered."

Suddenly a three-round burst from a subgun sounded over the cracks of the automatic pistols.

"Shit! They've found heavier artillery," Gadgets muttered.

The rattle from the subgun caused another burst of pistol fire. Then the submachine gun spoke again. Both Lao and Gadgets recognized its voice. They looked at each other.

"Only a mini-Uzi stutters that fast," Gadgets said.

"No bullets overhead," Lao observed.

She was right. The owners of the automatic pistols were too busy dueling with the Uzi to keep Lao and Schwarz pinned. Gadgets nodded, and they both sprang over the lip of the depression in opposite directions.

A few shots were sent their way, but they were hastily aimed. Gadgets rolled and scrambled for a boulder two feet from the depression where he had just been trapped. Spanish-made .32 slugs chewed ground just behind him.

Lao rolled to her feet and went into a squat eight feet from the edge of the shallow shelter. She took a two-handed grip on the MAC-11 and sent 9 mm debating points back toward the owners of the Llama Small Frames.

The Russian athletes found that their compact weapons were no match for the faster, stronger, more accurate punching of the three subguns facing them. They quietly crawled backward, keeping up a covering fire, but concentrating more on escape than on hitting targets.

The Stony Man warriors held their positions, sending only the occasional burst of fire to speed the Russian evacuation. It would be suicidal to try to track down the Russians. The rough land offered too many potential ambush locations.

Lao Ti, Gadgets and Blancanales slowly came out of their combat crouches and looked around.

"You two shouldn't stop for a romp in the field. We've work to do," Blancanales complained.

Lao shrugged. "You seem to manage okay."

"I saw the motorcycle and then heard the shots. So I left the press truck. Where's Ironman?"

"Trying to keep up with Cowley long enough to keep him alive until we find the rest of the Russians," Gadgets answered.

"Looks like you found them."

"They had a trap all set up for us. But they did get the body out of sight before anyone else saw it. I guess the police still don't know how serious things are."

"How are we going to find them now?" Pol asked.

"We're not. We've got to get to Cowley before Ironman kills himself. He's about ready to drop," Gadgets said.

"There's one motorcycle and three of us," Lao pointed out.

"Come on. We'll do something about that."

Gadgets led the way back to the road and the pile of bicycles. None of the cycles were usable. While the other two guarded him from snipers, Gadgets followed Lyons's example and pieced one together. It was a simple chore; racing wheels are meant to be changed without tools.

LYONS WAS HAVING TROUBLE with his breathing. The heat was oppressive, and the wind had died. It was the time of day when the wind started shifting from offshore to onshore.

Lyons found himself lifting his ass from the bicycle seat more and more to allow himself to stretch his back muscles and fully extend his legs. In spite of the difficulties, he managed to stay just two lengths behind Cowley. If he rode any closer, he would be disqualified for drafting.

There was still no sign of the Russians, and that bothered him. If they had given up the race, it was because they had something else in mind. He was simply too exhausted to figure out what the else could be.

The chanting was still following him along the last stretch of the race. Each group of people he passed started chanting, "Lono, Lono, Lono." The rhythm was beginning to penetrate his subconscious. He barely realized that he was pedaling in time to the chant.

He sucked on a dry water bottle and threw it away in disgust. The last aid station before changing over to the marathon footrace was just ahead. He had a bottle of Gatorade waiting there. He also had a couple of high-energy bars in the bag waiting for him. He wondered vaguely how he could have been so foolish as to imagine he would last this long.

Lyons drifted into a period of unconsciousness. He had no idea how long it lasted, but when he came to the aid station was in sight. He was still pedaling in time to the chanting. "Lono, Lono, Lono." It filled his head like echoes in a cave.

He pulled to a halt at the aid station and used wet sponges to cool down. He put the new bottle of liquid into the clip on the frame of the cycle and drank two cups of plain water. The chanting died away. As the chanting faded, he regained full consciousness.

He looked around for Cowley just in time to see him pulling away from the supply table. With a curse, Lyons applied himself to the pedals and started after the CIA target. Lyons's legs protested the lower gear. He shifted up as quickly as he could, preferring a hard, slow push to the rapid pumping of sore muscles.

As he slowly picked up speed, the chanting began again. "Lono, Lono, Lono." It rang in his head like great church bells. It pulsed through his veins like fresh blood. Without realizing it, he was exerting more energy.

As he munched the high-glucose bars and sipped Gatorade, he maintained his distance behind Cowley. When he finished, he returned both hands to the handgrips and closed the gap.

Cowley looked back. He seemed surprised to find Lyons behind him, smiling his grimace of pain and effort. The CIA man could no longer stand the sight of the Able Team warrior. He was an upstart who hadn't even trained for the race. He should be dead.

In a sudden burst of rage, Cowley whipped his bike to one side. Lyons had to veer to avoid an accident. He found himself off the road. The chanting suddenly turned into hisses and boos.

Cowley smiled, but when he looked ahead he found himself being waved down by a race official. Cowley squeezed the brakes, his mind leaping to some excuse, some defense that would keep him in the race.

An ancient stake truck from the 1960s, now doing duty as a press vehicle, accelerated and overtook him. The stake sides had been removed and about ten reporters and photographers were crouched on the flatbed. They seemed anxious to find out about the rule infraction. Cowley, in his frustration, had forgotten that from Kona onward there was no stretch without spectators and press.

"What seems to be the trouble?" Cowley asked.

"You're disqualified. Off road," the official shouted.

"What for?"

The official ignored the question. "Off road," he repeated.

"I have the right to know what for and who you are. I'm protesting this decision."

Several of the men on the press truck jumped down and crowded around them. Cowley turned to them for support.

"I have the right to know why I'm being forced out of the race and by whom. Isn't that right?"

No one answered. They were looking at him in the way a hungry fox looks at a plump chicken. Only then did Cowley realize he had been stopped by a Russian and that he was looking for support from the Russian press corps.

Sheltered from the spectators' sight by journalists, a photographer pulled a Makarov from his camera bag and jammed it into Cowley's side. The Bostonian decided that further debate was useless. The Russians closed ranks around him and hustled him onto the back of the open truck. As far as any witnesses were concerned, the journalists had decided to give a ride to a disqualified contestant who was too upset to think for himself.

As the truck pulled away, the smiling judge with the atrocious English picked up Cowley's cycle and prepared to wheel it out of sight. The crowd roared a warning, but he was unable to interpret it. He started to look around, but before he could see what all the fuss was about he was struck on the back of the neck. First there was a blinding explosion of light, then he slipped into unconsciousness.

Lyons didn't stop to examine the Russian official. He didn't even spare him a backward glance. Ironman pushed like hell on the pedals, trying to keep the Russian press truck in sight until other members of Able Team could arrive.

They would have to be quick. He was too exhausted to stay on the bicycle much longer.

## 21

It was a ridiculous way to catch up to Ironman, and it certainly wasn't efficient. But as long as Able Team stayed out of the way of the contestants, the race officials seemed disinclined to prevent the crazy journalists from doing what they wanted.

Blancanales drove the motorcycle, and Lao Ti rode the pillion sidesaddle with one arm around Pol's waist. Her other hand was stretched out to tow Gadgets, who rode the reconstructed bicycle.

The difficulty was that Lyons had already used the best front wheel from the tangle of bikes. There was a warp in the bicycle's front wheel that caused the bike to shimmy. Any speed over twenty miles an hour would have been fatal. Sweat stood out on Gadgets's forehead as he fought to keep the bike upright with one hand while he was pulled along with the other.

When Gadgets saw a neglected bike lying beside an unconscious race official in the middle of the road, it was too much of a temptation to pass up. He let go of Lao's hand and switched bikes while the crowd cheered.

The new bicycle was in perfect shape, and the Stony Man warriors resumed their journey at a better speed, pulling away from the scene just as an official car drove up to look into the matter. Fortunately the race officials decided to tend to the unconscious man before they pursued the clowns with the motorcycle towing the bicycle.

As the trio made its way along crowd-lined Alii Drive, a strange, rhythmic roaring grew louder. It soon became apparent that the crowd was chanting, "Lono, Lono, Lono." The sound moved from one section to the next.

Twelve miles from Kona Surf Resort, they overtook Lyons, who was red in the face and pumping the cycle as if he was chasing the devil himself. The chanting was focused on Lyons's furious effort. When he saw Able Team, he coasted and pointed at the Russian press truck.

"They got Cowley," was all Lyons was able to gasp.

The *spetsnaz* had known not to bolt the moment they snatched Cowley. They confined him in their midst while those on the outside continued to perform as if they were members of the press covering a sports event. The truck cruised past the racers at a speed slightly faster than the contestants. Several "journalists" sat on the edge of the flatbed, idly snapping photographs of the athletes they passed.

Blancanales put on a burst of speed that threatened to dump Gadgets on his ass. Somehow Schwarz managed to keep his balance while they streaked up to the press truck at fifty miles per hour. Gadgets's efforts were causing both the bicycle and the motorcycle to wobble. Here and there the crowd's chanting broke into howls of laughter.

Lyons was left pedaling furiously, determined to overtake the truck by sheer guts alone. It tore him to see the rest of the team going into action without him. His legs flashed to the steady rhythm of "Lono, Lono, Lono."

The Russians were so pleased with their success that they didn't take the trio sharing the bicycle and motorcycle seriously until it was too late. Blancanales came up directly behind the truck, but it wasn't until they were within a hundred yards that someone on the truck recognized them and shouted an alarm.

Gadgets and Lao Ti released their grip, which allowed Gadgets to glide up the right side of the slowly moving truck. Blancanales swerved and drove up the left side. In the heat of the day, the windows of the truck cab were down. Lao Ti pointed past Politician's head toward the cab. He nodded and gunned the motorcycle.

Gadgets made for the passenger door. The driver put the pedal to the floor, but the truck was old and picked up speed with a great deal of coughing and sputtering. The Stony Man warrior put his mettle to his pedals and overtook the cab just as the truck's speed reached his own. Gadgets threw himself sideways and grabbed the door with both hands, leaving the bicycle to fall on the road.

He swung his feet onto the running board just in time to come face-to-face with a Makarov that was held by the *spetsnaz* agent riding shotgun.

Blancanales matched speed with the accelerating truck. Lao Ti raised her feet to the running board, then grabbed the edge of the open window and pulled herself up. Her MAC-11 came out of its leg clip and nuzzled the driver's ear before he knew he had an extra passenger. He slammed on the brakes in an effort to dislodge her.

Momentum swung Lao forward. She put her weight behind the gun barrel, forcing it into the driver's ear and pushing his head to the right. Her right hand kept its grip on the door. Her left shoulder pressed into the large outside mirror and helped her keep her hold.

The driver let go of the wheel in his attempt to escape the pain of the gun barrel boring into his ear. The foot on the brake increased its pressure. The truck hadn't reached a high speed. It did a quarter turn and stopped before hitting the crowd.

Cyclists flashed by behind Lao, cursing the driver. The *spetsnaz* holding the automatic was slammed toward the dashboard by the sudden application of the brakes. His hands instinctively flew to the dashboard to prevent him from hitting his head. Gadgets used his right hand to pin the

Russian's gun hand to the dash. He held on frantically with his left until the truck came to a stop.

When he was able to release his grip on the door, Gadgets's left arm snaked in through the open window to wrap itself around the gunman's neck. He dragged the man's head out the window and started crushing the neck against the bottom window edge. A *spetsnaz* launched himself off the back of the truck and tackled Gadgets.

Blancanales drove straight ahead until he was well clear of the truck. When he was certain the vehicle couldn't ram him, he locked the brakes on the front wheel and gunned the engine. The bike slid through 180 degrees and powered out of the turn, headed for the now still truck.

He turned in time to see Cowley deliver a backhand smash to a Russian throat and then leap from the truck. Three *spetsnaz* pursued him. One started to reach for something under his left arm, looked at the crowd and checked himself. He shouted a warning in Russian, then the three killers started to hotfoot it after their prey.

Blancanales gave the cycle more gas and quickly overtook the CIA information prize.

"Jump on," he shouted in Cowley's ear.

E-4 gave him a startled look but did what he was told. The Able Team warrior roared away before Cowley was fully braced. The CIA man had to fight to keep from falling from the back of the motorcycle.

"Stop!" Cowley shouted. "Stop."

His voice carried such agony that Blancanales thought he had been shot. Politician spun the bike to put his body between the enemy and Cowley and then came to a full stop to examine how badly the man was wounded.

"My bike!" Cowley yelled. "My handmade import."

Cowley's bicycle was still undamaged, lying back on the road where it had fallen after Gadgets's wild leap to the truck.

Cowley jumped from the motorcycle and ran back for his bicycle. Blancanales cursed all stupid heroes and gunned the cycle after him.

Lao Ti withdrew the gun barrel from the Russian's damaged ear and then drove the gun forward again. The end of the barrel slammed into the driver's skull just behind the ear, knocking him unconscious. Lao leapt from the running board to face the Russian "newsmen" who were vaulting from the flatbed and charging her.

She couldn't see any weapons in their hands. They weren't so stupid as to brandish guns in front of an American crowd. She gauged her time, then bent down and returned her weapon to its leg clip.

She was still bent over when the first *spetsnaz* killer attacked. He lashed out with his foot, intending to drop-kick her head a hundred yards up the highway.

Lao moved her upper body to one side, allowing the foot to swing past her shoulder. Then she straightened, catching the back of his leg on her forearm. It was the dropkicker's head that bounced on the blacktop. Lao still had the leg over her forearm, holding his hips clear of the pavement. She took the time to place a kick of her own into his tailbone before dropping him.

The crowd had lost interest in the race and had become engrossed in the epic battle of the Pravda press truck. They yelled a warning as two more *spetsnaz* took flying tackles at Lao.

When Gadgets was tackled, he was forced to release his grip on the Russian's head and throat. He let the tackler's momentum carry them both to the pavement, but he twisted in the air so that they landed on the tackler's back and not his own.

The *spetsnaz* had the wind knocked from him, but he knew enough not to slacken his hold. There was no way he could defend himself if Gadgets escaped his hold.

Gadgets didn't have time to pry his hips loose from the tackler's embrace before two more Russians charged him. Gadgets rolled his shoulders against the pavement; his hips were still held firmly by the man under him. He bent both legs and sent a double-barreled blast of feet into the face of the first *spetsnaz* to reach him.

The force of the blow sent the man flying back into the front fender of the truck. His nose was flattened against his face.

The next *spetsnaz* was introduced to Gadgets's feet on the backswing. One boot caught the Russian on the side of the face, smashing his jaw. As the man staggered, the *spetsnaz* on the bottom of the heap realized that he was simply acting as a tripod to hold up Gadgets's lethal legs. He released his grip, which allowed Gadgets to do a shoulder roll out of the line of attack. Gadgets regained his feet, ready for the next onslaught. By this time he was surrounded.

Lao Ti stepped into the double attack, moving between the two GRU-trained goons. She grabbed two of their wrists and exerted pressure with her thumbs on the back of their hands, doubling them down toward the inside of the wrist. The two large Russians thought they had stuck their arms into leg traps. The pain was excruciating.

Lao continued to press ahead, forcing the two men to do an inside turn. The crowd roared its delight at seeing the two large bullies grimace in pain. Lao plunged straight ahead, forcing the Russians into the first few steps of a run. Then she stopped suddenly and reversed directions. The two *spetsnaz* slammed their heads together. The alternative was to have their wrists broken.

Lao let go and leaped clear, ready for the next attack. At that moment Cowley flashed past on his bicycle, completely ignoring Able Team and the Russians.

Two of the Russians reacted quickly to the situation. They crouched to spring on the cyclist as he passed. But as they launched themselves, a motorcycle roared in and intercepted their plan. The two Russians, Rosario Blancanales and the motorcycle all went down in a heap.

The Russian killers surrounding Gadgets promptly forgot him and leaped on the press truck as it began to move. Little Friedrich Vorovski had avoided the battle but had now taken over as driver. When he saw Cowley streak past, he put the truck in gear and started the pursuit. The Russians left the battle to jump aboard and continue after their main target.

Able Team found themselves in the middle of the road being cheered by the crowd while the *spetsnaz* sped off. As they ran for the motorcycle, Lyons puffed by, once again in the position of having to keep an eye on Cowley until the rest of the team took over.

Lyons had been left behind when Blancanales had towed Lao and Gadgets in their wobbly pursuit of the Pravda press truck. The truck had been brought to a stop a half mile ahead of him. In strained frustration, he had pushed against the hated bicycle pedals, knowing a battle was unfolding.

Lyons had seen Cowley make his break and cursed him for choosing to continue the race instead of helping his liberators. Technically Cowley should have disqualified himself. He had ridden in the truck for nearly six miles while Lyons had strained to keep the truck in sight—something he couldn't have done if the Russians hadn't gone slowly to preserve their cover.

When at last Lyons had reached the battle scene, the fight was over and the Russians had scrambled back onto the flatbed to continue their pursuit of Cowley. Lyons kept going, hoping that the rest of Able Team would quickly reach Cowley and force him from the race. The blond warrior streaked past the truck before it shifted to second, and pushed furiously ahead to join the Russians' target.

The crowd turned their attention back to the race, and once again the chant "Lono, Lono, Lono," followed Lyons.

The race officials and police had reacted slowly. They hadn't known what to make of the disturbance involving the Russian press, and they were unwilling to do anything that might escalate into an international incident.

They were relieved when it seemed to break up of its own accord. The race officials made note of the unusual press team on the motorcycle and bicycle. They would be barred from future races. They had been so worried about the fight that Cowley's transition from press truck to bicycle had escaped them.

Gadgets found himself without transportation. Blancalanes and Lao took off after Cowley and the *spetsnaz*. Cowley had taken the bicycle that Gadgets had been using. He had no choice but to jog toward Kona Surf and hope that the rest could handle whatever came up. Already the top athletes were running past him in the opposite direction. They were headed toward the final finish line.

Blancanales and Lao couldn't overtake the press truck. The *spetsnaz* had grouped at the back of the truck bed. The two in the middle, concealed from the crowd by their comrades, leveled handguns at the motorcycle. Politician hung back to avoid pistol range. He would wait until the Russian kidnappers had to divide their attention between Able Team and Cowley. That was the time to make his move. By then Cowley might have reached the transition point and would be protected by his own men.

Lyons was perplexed when the Russian truck didn't overtake him and when Able Team didn't overtake the Russians. He had no idea what was holding things up. He could only hope that whatever it was would resolve itself soon; he didn't know how much farther he could go.

The chant from the crowd was once again overwhelming his exhausted body and mind. "Lono, Lono, Lono." His body soaked up the rhythm and began to move to it. "Lono, Lono, Lono." The agony of pain and the torment of the mission drowned in the mesmerizing beat of the chant.

"Lono, Lono, Lono." Lyons's mind closed and left the chant and the body to do as they would.

He was totally unaware that the press truck had stopped following him.

**22**

Lyons moved rhythmically to the chant that filled him completely. "Lono, Lono, Lono." He was unaware of hoisting his ass high off the bicycle seat, of stretching and loosening knotted muscles.

Just ahead of him, Cowley finally stopped and dismounted from his bike. Lyons was so relieved that he simply let his own bike drop when he pulled up to the CIA's. He staggered after the briefing officer until he was surrounded by a group of giggling Hawaiian women. He shook his head to clear away the illusion.

Shaking his head didn't work. He was eased onto a stool by many small hands. Women's voices whispered, "Let me help Lono." Small hands sponged his burning skin and then spread soothing lotion on all the exposed areas. Someone removed his cycling shoes and put something else on his feet. Other hands brought him cool water. He drank several cups, thinking he would ask questions once his thirst was assuaged.

But when he was finished drinking, his thoughts turned to the visor that had been placed on his head. It had a handkerchief glued on the back. It vaguely rang a bell, but he couldn't quite place it.

Then he was pulled to his feet and found himself looking out of a tent at a blacktop road that shimmered in the heat of the late afternoon sun. The gale force winds had died to nothing. Soon the first traces of the evening onshore breezes would stir the foliage. For the present, things were uncomfortably still.

Someone thrust a plastic bag into his hand and gave him a timid shove. Lyons saw food in the bag. He didn't recognize it as his own transition bag, but his body saw food and cried out its need. His legs started moving as he put the first fig to his mouth.

Immediately the chant began again. "Lono, Lono, Lono." Lyons legs picked up the rhythm with giant strides. He was oblivious to the applause all around him. Only the "Lono, Lono, Lono" seeped into his soul, propelling him over the endless blacktop.

Lyons munched a glucose candy while his fogged mind wrestled with the greatest problems of the universe. What was little Carl Lyons doing? Why was he running down an endless highway lined with palm trees and strange voices? What were the voices saying?

He started on another fig. He should be able to answer the last question. What were the voices saying? Lyons looked down at his feet. They seemed blurred and far away. He knew he wasn't moving them, but who was? He knew then that the voices were moving his feet.

Lyons also saw the empty plastic bag in his hands. Why was he carrying an empty bag? He could see no reason for it; so he tossed the bag away. His hands started to pump, and his feet moved even faster.

Suddenly a tent and table intruded on his consciousness. Lyons accepted two Styrofoam cups from a blurred but smiling face. He drank the water from one and dumped the contents of the other on his head. He was burning up, and the water felt good.

Before he had been given the water he had been thinking profound thoughts, solving the riddles of the universe, considering questions of huge importance. But what were the questions? What was he doing here? Yes, that was the question. What was he doing here? That rhythmic noise, the chanting, made thinking so much easier. He was after Cowley. He had to pull him from the race. Cowley was somewhere ahead.

He knew he had run through a town, but he couldn't associate it with anywhere. He had run on open highway. At one of the places where they had put food and water into his hands, they had turned him around. At least he thought they had turned him around. It seemed as if the dying sun had been on his other shoulder.

Lyons raised his eyes, but very little registered. There were a few faceless runners staggering toward him. A runner just ahead who wasn't Cowley. A blur of faces along each side of the road. And a noise, a steady beat of a noise that kept his feet moving. "Lono, Lono, Lono."

Lyons's feet moved faster, oblivious to the tortured pull of his lungs. He had something to do, and it was up ahead. What was ahead? Two people with armbands were looking at him strangely. As he approached, he could hear one shout to the other over the roar of the crowd.

"We should pull him from the race. He's not going to live to the finish line."

"Better not," the other figure cautioned. "He's allowed to keep going until he drops. Besides, the crowd might turn on us."

Then Lyons was past them, wondering who they were talking about. Probably Cowley. He had to catch up with Cowley before he killed himself. Lyons ran faster.

WHEN THE RUSSIAN TRUCK STOPPED, Blancanales slowed down, not wanting to overtake them until he knew what was happening. The men leaped from the back and started clearing spectators from an intersection. By the time Pol and Lao reached the spot, the truck had turned inland and was speeding away from the race. Spectators had moved into the intersection again, effectively closing it to traffic.

Blancanales had to make an instant decision: should he follow the truck or try to find Lyons and Cowley? He had the Russians in sight. It would be safer to stick with them.

Lao pushed back the crowd in an effort to make room for Politician to wheel the motorcycle through. But everyone was eagerly waiting for Lono to run past on the final leg of the race, and they paid little attention to the two people trying to pass through their midst.

Lao was forced to send her elbows and thumbs into people's ribs and stomachs. She cleared a path, but by the time they got the cycle past the human barrier the Russians had a head start. They sped after the truck, surprised at how much speed the driver could coax out of the old monster.

They saw the truck take a dirt road that headed north. They wheeled the corner cautiously in case of an ambush, but the driver was going as fast as he could on the rough road. The men in the back were all standing where they could hang on to the stake frame that remained on the bed. It was all the Russians could do to keep from being bounced off.

Politician had trouble on the loose gravel. He could keep the truck in sight, but was unable to overtake it. Lao hung on to his hips with a grip that felt like steel claws biting into his flesh.

The dusty chase took them onto Highway 11. The truck picked up speed, but Blancanales also started to gain. The truck flashed through built-up areas, indifferent to the danger to residents. Luckily most people were watching the race, and the truck was so noisy that the few pedestrians in the area managed to scramble out of the way in time.

The truck cleared the path, and Politician followed. He hung back far enough to discourage the *spetsnaz* on the truck bed from taking up target practice.

The chase flashed by the east end of Kona and started in land on Highway 190

Lao wrapped one arm around Blancanales's waist and used the other hand to fish for her communicator. She tried it several times but couldn't raise Gadgets. She finally decided her unit was no longer functional. She began the frustrating job of trying to return it to her belt clip with one hand. It took a while.

There was little traffic and no sign of the police. The sun set, and the short twilight deepened quickly.

They were getting close to the Waimea Kohala Airport and Highway 19. The Russian driver waited until he turned onto another unpaved road before turning on his headlights. The roughness and the twisting course of the road made the lights essential.

Lao managed to replace her unit but couldn't spare a hand to reach for Politician's. The road was as rough as the other unpaved road they had been on. She knew Gadgets would be trying to reach them.

The truck took another sharp turn onto a road that doubled back toward Highway 19 and eventually into Kona. Blancanales whipped around the corner ninety seconds behind the truck to find that he had driven straight into an ambush.

GADGETS HADN'T JOGGED more than a hundred yards before he was stopped by a race official who demanded he get off the road.

"Press," Gadgets said.

"Show me your pass," the official countered.

Gadgets was frustrated and angry. The rest of the team probably needed him, and he was going to be forced into the crowd where he would be unable to move even at a walk. Gadgets had an overwhelming urge to push the official out of the way and to continue running. The urge stopped him. The man was only doing his job. It would do little good to take out his frustration on an innocent party.

Gadgets smiled and faded into the crowd, but inwardly he was seething. The anger was now turned against himself and his sense of failure. He berated himself for letting the team down.

Gadgets took out his communicator and tried to raise Lao Ti or Blancanales without success. He was frowning when he returned the radio to his button-down shirt pocket.

A slow increase in the crowd noise brought Gadgets out of his frustrated self-condemnation. He had heard that sound too much to ever forget it. Even before he could make out the words, he knew the crowd was shouting for Lono. Ironman was actually returning!

Gadgets fought his way back to the edge of the crowd and stepped out onto the street just in time to see Lyons run by. Gadgets couldn't believe how well he was running. He had been barely alive during the last part of the bike race.

There was an angry shout and screech of brakes. A race official on a motor scooter stopped to escort Gadgets off the road again, but Gadgets paid no attention. He was staring open-mouthed as Cowley ran past. Cowley was running behind Lyons! What was happening? The race official was shouting louder, but Gadgets didn't pay him the slightest attention. His only thought was to cover Lyons and Cowley until Pol and Lao showed up.

He reached over and steadied the official's motor scooter with his left hand. With his right, he grabbed the angry official by bunching his T-shirt at the back. Then he lifted the small man clear of the scooter and set him down on the pavement. The official struggled and swore, pulling himself out of the T-shirt.

Gadgets ripped off his safari jacket, unconcerned that his businesslike MAC-10 showed to the whole crowd. He threw his jacket to the surprised man and put on the official T-shirt of the race organizers. Then he threw the scooter into gear and rode off, leaving the unharmed official staring after him.

Gadgets was soon clear of the crowd that had witnessed the clothing exchange. No one questioned his right to patrol the race. He increased his speed in an effort to catch up to Cowley. If Lyons thought he should lead the way, he knew what he was doing. Gadgets was content to follow.

From where he followed Cowley, Gadgets could hear the chanting, "Lono, Lono, Lono," from somewhere ahead. It always died out before Cowley caught up with it.

Officials were handing green chemical light rods to each runner. It was compulsory to carry them after dark. The runners held them like batons. It would make an interesting sight when the darkness was complete.

Gadgets hadn't seen Blancanales or Lao for more than two hours. Were they ahead of Lyons? He drove the scooter with one hand and tried his communicator, but again he received no answer. Ahead of him, Cowley was beginning to wobble as he ran, adding extra steps to the 26.2-mile marathon.

The hours passed, and Gadgets grew increasingly agitated. Several times he stopped and wheeled the scooter into the crowd when he saw the glow of approaching headlights. Cars would go by slowly, looking at everyone wearing an official T-shirt.

After the third delay, Gadgets left the scooter on the road where it would be found and started to jog behind his charge. He knew he could outlast Cowley easily at this point. But where in hell was the rest of the team?

ROSARIO BLANCANALES REACTED automatically. Hundreds of dangerous situations had conditioned his body to react before his mind had time to fully comprehend the danger. Without that conditioning, none of the Able Team warriors could have survived.

He aimed the bike at the right-hand ditch and twisted the accelerator. The *spetsnaz* had left the truck in sight; they hadn't known it would alert and bring an instant reaction from their quarry. The ambushers were holding their fire, waiting for an effective cross fire situation that would never happen.

The motorbike dipped into the ditch, out the other side and sped across a rough lava field. Blancanales and Lao were in as much danger from his driving as they were from the handgun fire behind them. When they were out of effective range, Politician slowed down allowing Lao to jump off. Then he turned the cycle in a large arc that would take him back to the road in front of the truck.

The Russian killers were less than delighted to find their intended ambush victims outflanking them. The need for concealed weapons had limited them to automatics, and they knew from experience that the two warriors would have better weapons. Even though it was eight Russians to two Able Team members, the *spetsnaz* didn't like the odds. They broke position and ran for the truck.

As they ran, they kept up a trickle of fire to hold Politician and Lao at a distance. The terrain grew rougher and rockier. Blancanales tried to get enough speed to reach the road before the Russians could reach the truck. Instead, he hit a patch of loose rock and had to jump clear as the motorcycle spilled.

He hit the rocky ground hard and rolled. As he rolled, he heard a piece of equipment crack on a sharp rock. The Stony Man warrior was badly bruised and winded. The Russians saw the spill and instantly changed plans. It would be easy to wipe out a badly shaken opponent. They changed direction and spread out in a long line of skirmish, approaching the position where they saw the gray-haired warrior fall.

Pol rolled and scrambled for cover among the rocks, but there was no place that would protect him from several directions at once. He paused, fighting to regain his wind, knowing that he would need it. He tried to locate the Russians by sound, but he was breathing too heavily.

Lao saw Blancanales's plight and began a long run to bring her up behind the skirmish line. Someone who had stayed in the truck barked orders in Russian. Two of the *spetsnaz* broke off to keep between Lao and the rest of the killers. The skirmish line changed direction slightly, concentrating on a single point.

Even if Pol had realized what they were after, he could have done little to stop them. He lay in the rocks, his mini-Uzi ready, waiting for the first slip, the first lapse of attention that would give him a point to attack. He knew he couldn't stay where he was.

The Russians in the skirmish line suddenly opened up. It wasn't a wild barrage of fire but carefully spaced shots that allowed a few *spetsnaz* to reload at a time. Blancanales wondered why the bullets weren't coming closer.

He changed position and looked up quickly. Only one 7.62 mm invitation to death whined off a rock close to his head. The rest of the firing was directed at the point where he had originally abandoned the motorcycle.

Pol rolled again and popped up to fire a short burst. He missed. The Russians were retreating and had changed position.

Lao Ti was equally frustrated. Although her MAC-11 was superior to anything the Russians seemed to be carrying, she didn't have any ammunition to waste. Firing at the present range would soon leave her without bullets and would probably not account for more than one or two of the enemy. Somehow she had to distract them until Blancanales could start a countermove.

She broke into a run over the rough ground, trying to force more attention to herself and to give Pol a better break. But there was no confrontation. The *spetsnaz* kept retreating, doing only enough shooting to keep her wary.

Then Blancanales broke cover on her right. He began to move in on the Russians as fast as he could scramble from one piece of cover to the next. But he didn't really understand the situation; it was the Russians who should be attacking.

The *spetsnaz* converged on their press truck and jumped onto the back. They kept a slow but steady trickle of fire directed at Pol and Lao.

The two Stony Man warriors opened up with short bursts, but the range was extreme. The Russians went flat, and then the truck pulled away.

The weird shadows of dusk had settled across the field as Blancanales scrambled for the motorcycle. When he reached it, he stopped cold and then turned away.

It had been the chief target of the Russians' shooting. It wasn't going anywhere.

"Quick, your communicator. Mine's broken," Lao said.

Politician opened his belt pouch and pulled out his small radio. The case was broken. He had a handful of parts held together only by the wiring. Pieces of the case and a couple of parts fell into the darkness. The two Stony Man warriors were isolated from the other members of Able Team.

Lao sighed as she looked around. There were no buildings in sight.

"Have you a light?" she asked.

Blancanales produced a small flashlight.

"A pocketknife?"

Although Pol was not as infamous as Gadgets for having a pocketful of tools, he did have a small multipurpose knife.

Lao took out her communicator and patiently began to open it up. Every second counted, but she would lose time if she tried to hurry.

## 23

It seemed to Lyons that he had been running forever. There had never been a time when he wasn't inundated with voices chanting "Lono, Lono, Lono." Was that his name? Probably. He could remember no other name at the moment.

Somewhere along the way he had discarded whatever it was that he had been wearing on his head. Now and then someone would thrust a cup into his hand and he would drink. Occasionally he found a wet sponge in his hand and would cool his burning skin with it, then toss it away. He wasn't sure, but he thought he had been doing this all his life.

From time to time, someone in front of him would stagger and almost fall. Lyons himself wobbled as the onshore winds picked up in intensity. They weren't as strong as the winds had been during the bicycle race, but they were beginning to bother the runners.

It was dark, but streetlights lit his way. The crowd was thicker now and the chanting louder. He was passing buildings, but he couldn't focus his eyes to really see what they were.

Lyons knew he was running for a reason. He kept battering his exhausted mind until it remembered.

Someone named Cowley was in danger. He had to catch up to Cowley and protect him until others arrived. What others? He couldn't remember. He had to remember! He frowned with anger at his sluggish memory. The anger didn't help his recall ability, but it made his feet go faster.

The chant from the crowd picked up his new energy and grew in intensity. The water was now much closer on his left. The waves pounded the shore, their roaring adding to the din of the crowd. Lyons ran on, hearing only "Lono, Lono, Lono." The wind had become part of the experience. He no longer noticed it.

Then there were people milling all over the road ahead of him. He couldn't get through. He wove and dodged, knocking someone over. The chant had dissolved into a roar. People were whistling and clapping. But he couldn't get through. Suddenly two brawny men each grabbed one of his arms and raised him from the ground. Lyons's feet kept trying to run, churning the air.

"Easy," someone said. "You've finished. You've done it."

They were carrying him somewhere. But he had to catch up to Cowley.

"Got to keep going," he muttered.

"Boy, is he out of it!" someone else exclaimed. "Wonder why the judges didn't stop him?"

"He looked great coming down the last stretch. Can't always tell."

Lyons ignored the talk. He had something to do. What was it, again?

The two men carried him inside a tent. A muscular man said, "I'll take him at my table."

Through Lyons's haze he heard someone say, "Sure, Ululani, but no one's walked him. He's too out of it."

They sat Lyons down on a padded table. His legs were still trying to run, though they had now subsided to a regular, rhythmic twitching.

"Cowley," Lyons muttered. "Got to catch up to Cowley."

Mauna's voice said, "Cowley hasn't come in yet He's still running."

"Help me rub him down, Mauna. He hasn't been walked."

Four hands started torturing Lyons's twitching, screaming muscles.

Someone was bending over him, kneading his knotted shoulder muscles. The muscles were beginning to relax enough for the massage to feel good. Someone propped him up and put a cup of diluted Gatorade to his lips. He drank it greedily. Then the massage began again.

Lyons opened his eyes, but he was still having trouble focusing. Whoever was massaging his upper body wore a pendant on a chain around his neck. The pendant swung back and forth over Lyons's eyes. He strained to make out its shape.

It was a figure made of iron. It swung back and forth, in and out of his range of vision. It had his face! It winked at him. Lyons sighed and closed his eyes.

People moved in and out of the large tent, but the four hands kept rubbing, kneading and working his muscles. Periodically someone would pour more Gatorade in him. Lyons looked past the swinging medallion.

He said, "Hi, Mauna." His voice was hoarser than usual. It sounded like someone else's.

"You're back with us, are you? Congratulations."

"For what?"

"For finishing the triathlon. The *mumuku* was worse this year than during any other race. A lot of the athletes couldn't handle those winds at all, but you finished in the top third."

Before Lyons could assimilate what he was being told, two men helped another runner into the tent. The big man who had been massaging Lyons's back and legs looked up and grinned.

Lyons watched with detached curiosity as Ululani, his masseur, turned to the next table. Two men were supporting Cowley, who looked as spent as Lyons felt. However, when E-4 saw Lyons on the next massage table he balked.

"You!" he panted at Lyons. "You finished?"

Ululani helped stretch Cowley out.

"Twenty minutes ago," the Hawaiⁱan told Cowley in a cheerful voice.

The tall Bostonian seemed to wilt when he heard the news. The big masseur went to work on his muscles with cheerful vigor that made Cowley wince. As he worked, he kept up a line of chatter that did nothing to cheer his patient.

"I was just telling Mr. Lyons how you paid us to take care of his friends. We really did a number on them. Though, if we'd known they were going to be so tough, we probably would have charged you more."

"Shut up!" Cowley croaked.

He tried to get up to see if Lyons had taken this in, but Ululani pushed him back down.

"I want you to know we did a good job for you, sir. Three of them. One may not walk again. That should be worth a bonus, shouldn't it?"

Lyons was back in the world enough to understand what was being said. He glanced at Cowley, who was squirming from the pain of the verbal massage. All the time Ululani's talented hands soothed Cowley's muscles, the Hawaiian's words planted barbs in the CIA man's mind. Cowley was physically writhing on the massage table.

Lyons noticed something near the door. Gadgets was standing there, munching on a banana and smiling at Cowley's discomfort. Cowley hadn't spotted Gadgets.

"Shut up," Cowley ordered Ululani. "Are you trying to get us killed?"

He looked over at Lyons, who sat up and forced a grin.

"I'd better leave this spot for someone who needs it," he told Cowley. "Congratulations."

"Congratulations?" Cowley was mystified.

"You lived to finish the race," Lyons told him.

Ironman staggered out of the tent on his own. Gadgets was waiting just outside to drape Lyons's arm over his shoulder and steer him toward Sherrie Lilivokalani's car. Mauna caught up and supported Lyons from the other side. Lyons let him, although the Stony Man warrior no longer felt it was necessary.

"What happened?" Lyons asked.

They moved slowly out of the cordoned-off area to the place where vehicles waited to collect the athletes. As they went, Gadgets filled Ironman in on the events that had precipitated the now friendly relationship between Able Team and the Kapu'ukus.

Lyons managed a dry chuckle as he steered himself toward a black Mercedes that had someone behind the wheel and a couple of people in the back seat.

"Not that one," Gadgets said. "Over here."

Sherrie Lilivokalani and David Waihee were waiting beside the princess's car. Nikko had her Pinto parked right behind the black limousine. An anxious Jane Briggs was pacing up and down alongside both cars.

Sherrie strode to meet them and gave Lyons a victory kiss. Lyons clung tightly to keep from wobbling. The princess responded by extending the kiss. The rest of the group cheered.

Gadgets produced more Gatorade and some sweet figs, which Lyons tackled before he got into the car.

Jane stopped her pacing in front of Lyons.

"Where's Pol?" she demanded. Her voice was sharp, accusing.

Lyons shrugged, then turned to Gadgets.

"Where's Pol? Where's Lao?" Ironman demanded around a mouthful of half-chewed fig.

"They went after the Pravda truck. We haven't seen them or the Russians since," Gadgets reported.

"You're responsible," Jane spat at Lyons. "If you hadn't entered that silly race..."

Lyons ignored her, focusing his attention on Gadgets. "Give " he demanded. "Why no radio contact?"

Gadgets shrugged. Lyons could see that he was worried, but that he didn't want to say anything. There was no need to ask Gadgets if he had tried to raise them on the communicator. He would have done that before reporting to the massage tent.

The tense scene was interrupted by Cowley's arrival at the parking lot. He was trying to run, although he could do little more than stagger. The CIA officer was followed by a grinning Ululani, who twice prevented him from falling.

"Get away from me," Cowley shouted.

"Chee, boss," the big gang leader said, using a Chicago accent. "I'm just trying to see youse don't get rubbed out on the way home."

"Don't call me 'boss.'"

"But you hired me to do those guys in. Don't that make you my boss?"

"Shut up!"

"Sure, boss."

Cowley yanked open the door of the other Mercedes and demanded, "Why weren't you clowns at the finish line to cover me?"

A Llama Small Frame emerged from the car and was thrust under Cowley's chin.

"Get in." The voice behind the gun was as cold as the wind blowing across the Siberian wasteland.

"Ululani, get down!" Gadgets shouted.

The Hawaiian gang leader had the brains to respond first and ask questions later. Three .38 slugs bit through the back window of Cowley's car and chewed air where Ululani had been standing.

Cowley was yanked into the back seat of the Mercedes, which peeled rubber as it sped from the parking area.

"IT'S A HIGHWAY," Blancanales said needlessly. "Now, if we just knew which one, we could request taxi service."

It had taken Lao a while before she had located the defective part in her communicator. She had taken out the damaged tuning circuit and had substituted the board from Pol's broken communicator. There had been no way to solder the board in, so one of them had held it in place while the other had tried to get the device to work.

Pol and Lao had agreed to find out where they were before calling in. They weren't sure how long they could get the radio to function.

After fixing the communicator, the two Able Team warriors had made a trek to the closest point where they had seen light. The highway was unlit, but there was a filling station not far away. They had homed in on the station's lights.

Now they went into an office. One grumpy teenage pump attendant was the only person present. He seemed indifferent to their plight but helped them locate themselves on a map. Blancanales and Lao put the communicator parts on the counter. Lao held them together while Pol tried to raise Gadgets.

"Nothing," Pol reported. "You sure it's working?"

Lao carefully examined everything in the better light of the garage office. The teenager watched them with a smirk on his lips that said he thought he was dealing with a couple of idiots.

Three minutes later Lao said, "It's okay. Try again."

Pol again tried to summon Gadgets. The only response was static.

"Electrical tape," Lao demanded.

"This ain't a hardware store," the attendant said.

"Do you ever make bets?" Pol asked him.

The young man looked blank.

Pol reached in his pocket and pulled out a twenty-dollar bill.

"I'll bet you twenty dollars you can't find us a soldering iron and some electrician's tape."

"You'd win. The mechanics lock up their tools at night."

Politician had a good idea why they locked up their tools, but he kept a friendly smile on his face.

"Bet you twenty you can't even find tape."

"You're on."

The attendant disappeared into the mechanic's bay and quickly came back with a small roll of black plastic tape. He banged it on the counter, snatched the twenty and grinned.

Lao Ti patiently taped the connections into place.

"Try again," she ordered.

## 24

As Cowley's Mercedes pulled away, Gadgets's communicator beeped, but he couldn't take the time to answer it. Everyone was scrambling to pursue the Russians.

Lyons shoved Lilivokalani into the back seat of her car and scrambled in after her. Captain Waihee drove; Gadgets jumped in beside him. Mauna helped Ululani to his feet, and both men sprinted for the Pinto. Nikko was already in the driver's seat starting the engine.

Jane Briggs was left standing in the parking lot. She hadn't attempted to get into either car.

Cowley's Mercedes burst from the parking area, clearing people out of the way with its horn. The second Mercedes and the Pinto were close enough to take advantage of the cleared road. They fought their way beyond the crowds and followed Kalani Street out of town. After a few zigzags, they headed north on Highway 190.

Gadgets leaned out the open window and tried to raise Blancanales and Lao on the communicator. The only response he received was a bullet that snapped past his head, a present from the fleeing Mercedes. He hastily ducked back inside, leaving the short antenna outside the window.

Waihee started to swerve the car back and forth to discourage and frustrate the gunman in the car ahead. Gadgets's communicator beeped again, but he was off-balance and couldn't get his head to the built-in microphone.

"Drop back a bit so I can use the communicator," he shouted at Waihee.

The skipper let the distance between the cars increase by two hundred yards. They were out of the populated area and in little danger of losing Cowley's car. Gadgets hung out the window and tried again, without result.

"We can't hang back too long," Waihee said. "I don't want to lose sight of them in case they take an unmarked side road."

"Hang back as long as you can," Gadgets told him. "I want to be able to answer the next time this thing buzzes."

LAO TI WORKED CAREFULLY, methodically, checking that each connection was taped tightly. She knew seconds were precious, but rapid work left too much room for error. Blancanales watched her discipline with a mixture of awe and impatience. The gas attendant also watched Lao's every move; his was a look of sheer admiration.

"Try again," she told Pol.

This time, Gadgets's voice bounced right back. "Is that you, Pol?"

"Who were you expecting, your girlfriend?"

"Where are you?"

"Highway 19, about four miles east of Route 270."

"Stop joking around!" Gadgets's voice was angry.

"No joke. What's up?"

"They snatched Cowley in his own car. We're in pursuit and headed northeast along 190. Can you intercept? We'll probably lose them if they reach another crowded area. They don't care how many people they run down."

"No vehicle, but we'll do our damnedest."

"Keep in touch."

"Can't. Out."

Blancanales looked up at the gas jockey as Lao picked up the rebuilt communicator and carefully stuffed it into her pocket.

"I need transportation," Pol told the attendant.

The boy didn't take his eyes off Lao. "Try a taxi, mister."

Lao reached over and picked the teenager up by his shirt front.

"We need it now," she told him.

He tried a punch. She merely caught his hand and squeezed his fist. He turned white.

"Do I have your full attention?"

He nodded.

"Now."

Politician had been rummaging through the counter drawer while Lao dealt with the attendant.

"Found the tow truck keys," he announced.

Lao waited until Pol was back around the counter before letting the surly teenager drop back in his chair.

"That's theft. You'll go to jail," he shouted.

"Don't forget to call the police," Lao reminded him as she followed Politician out the door and toward the truck.

Pol pulled away as soon as Lao swung into the passenger seat. She pulled out the communicator and began checking it once more.

"I told them we wouldn't be in touch," Pol reminded her.

"Nothing better to do."

Pol had no answer to that and concentrated on getting them over to Highway 190.

The young man watched them drive off in the tow truck with the flashers blinking. He reached for the telephone. He had been hassled by the police before over some pot. He let go of the telephone. He would just tell the boss that he hadn't noticed that the truck was missing.

THE TURNOFF TO WAIKOLOA GOLF COURSE was getting closer, and Waihee stepped on the gas. The Mercedes rocketed forward, gaining slowly on the car ahead. Waihee's driving forced Gadgets to yank his head and communicator back inside the car window. He was now sure that a pleasure cruise with the skipper would be an adventure worth missing.

Cowley's car suddenly took a sharp right toward the golf course. Gadgets hung on as Waihee powered through the change in direction, deliberately spinning the back wheels to complete the turn in time.

They sped past the golf course toward Highway 19.

"Damn!" Gadgets said to no one in particular. "Now Pol's going the wrong way to head them off."

Gadgets glanced back to check on the Pinto and then on Ironman. The Pinto was losing ground to the more powerful cars, but its headlights were still in sight. Ironman was asleep. He had his head on Sherrie's lap. She was looking down on him with a tender smile that transformed her strong face. Gadgets quickly turned just as his communicator beeped.

He stuck his head out the window, but the noise from the wind was too high. He finally managed to get only the antenna through the window and was able to angle the rest of the communicator so that he could still use it.

"Yeah," he shouted into the radio.

Lao's voice came back, clearly, calmly. "We're headed south on 190."

Gadgets had to hang on as they swerved north again.

When he was able to answer, he said, "No use. We've cut over to 19 and are headed north along the coast."

He heard Blancanales swear in the background.

"We'll do what we can," Lao said with a calm voice.

The pursuit continued through marsh lands and past Kiholo. Few people were around, and the cars sped on without incident. They were rapidly approaching a branch in the highway.

"Drop back," Gadgets warned Waihee. "Things are going to get hairy in a couple of minutes."

"Your friends won't make it," Waihee predicted.

"Drop back."

Waihee shook his head, but did as Gadgets said.

They shot through Puako doing ninety miles an hour. The Pinto was a half mile back, but keeping up. They were almost to the point where Highway 19 turned inland and Highway 270 continued north when the taillights of the lead car flashed bright. Beyond them they could see the amber flashers of a tow truck.

Cowley's Mercedes, driven by a Russian, fishtailed and then turned nearly 180 degrees before coming to a stop. Waihee hit the brakes and brought the other limousine to a much smoother stop. Then he turned it sideways so that it blocked most of the highway.

The sudden deceleration woke Lyons, who had slept through the rocking, swerving chase. He sat up, rubbing his eyes and looking groggy. Gadgets pulled Lyons's Python from his backpack and handed it over the seat. Then he passed over three speed loaders. Lyons had left his mesh jacket behind and didn't have any pockets in his triathlon suit. He waved away the speed loaders.

When the car stopped, Gadgets and Sherrie Lilivokalani shot out of the side nearest the enemy and made for the left-hand ditch. Waihee and Lyons scrambled into the opposite ditch. The Pinto stopped farther back. Nikko, Mauna and Ululani watched to see what would happen next.

Lyons remembered this part of the highway from his practice sessions and from the bicycle part of the triathlon. During the day, the ruins of Puukohola Heiau, the Temple on the Hill of the Whale, would be visible on his right. In the darkness, the area was lit with many torches and candles. The wind carried the sound of chanting from that direction.

The Russians found themselves sandwiched between the known danger of Lyons and Gadgets at the limousine and the unknown danger of the occupants of the tow truck. They chose to take on whoever was with the tow truck.

Three of them advanced cautiously, but quickly turned back when they were greeted by the high-speed fire of subguns.

The entire group of Russians took off across the lava flows toward the waving candles and torches. Two of the *spetsnaz* agents propelled Cowley's lanky form between them.

"They probably hope to lose us in the crowd," Gadgets shouted across the road to Lyons.

"It's certainly going to neutralize our weapons," Lyons answered. "Let's go."

The two warriors stood up and started to follow the Russians. Two figures walked away from the tow truck and began to move in on the Russians' flank. They didn't hurry. The Russians would beat them to the crowd at the temple anyway. They would use the worshippers as hostages. That much was plain.

The Hawaiians moved the vehicles and unblocked the road before following Able Team. The tall princess linked her arm through Ululani's and strode across the field, with Waihee, Nikko and Mauna all half running to keep up with them.

Ahead, the chanting suddenly became profound silence as the Russians thrust their prisoner through the outer fringes of the crowd. As Able Team closed in, they could see over a hundred people gathered for the re-creation of the ancient ritual.

*"Kapu. Kapu!"* several voices called as the Russians pushed their way onto the sacred ground.

The *spetsnaz* didn't pause. They shoved and threatened with their handguns until they were in the center of the holy area, a spot where only the priest was allowed. He stood silent but glared at them.

Lilivokalani caught up with Able Team just as they reached the outskirts of the group. She touched Lyons on the shoulder.

"What will you do?" she asked.

"Stop them, now. E-4 has enough information in his head to cost us many more lives than I see here." His voice was profoundly tired, but it carried over the hushed audience.

"You will not stop us," Vorovski called to Lyons. "We will be picked up here, and you do not have what it takes to cause the deaths of so many innocent people." The small man gloated with victory.

The priest, or leader, spoke for the first time. "You have already defiled ground we hold sacred. Do not also shed blood on it. Blood will awaken the god of war who sleeps here."

Vorovski answered him with a snort of derision.

On the highway, a semitrailer had pulled to a stop by the parked vehicles. The Russian grinned in the torchlight.

"Here comes our transportation now."

Able Team saw the pattern immediately. It was a simple one. Half the surviving *spetsnaz* had overpowered Cowley's guards and waited for him in his car. The other half had somehow secured a semitrailer. If Able Team hadn't taken up the chase immediately, Cowley's Mercedes would have been driven into the trailer and simply disappeared.

Still grinning, Vorovski fired his weapon into the air twice. The headlights of a passing car silhouetted six forms as they leaped from the tractor-trailer and started across the field toward the assembled group.

"Stop them," Lyons told Able Team.

Gadgets nodded toward the group holding Cowley. "What about them?"

"I'll take care of them."

Gadgets looked at the exhausted slump of Lyons's shoulders and hesitated.

"Do it!" Lyons barked.

Gadgets looked at him for several seconds, weighing, evaluating, then he turned and jogged to meet the new threat. Blancanales and Lao Ti followed him, spreading out as they ran over the treacherously dark field.

Lyons held up his Python for all to see, then turned and handed it to Sherrie. He started to walk toward the Russians.

*"Kapu, kapu,"* several worshippers muttered.

It looked as if the Hawaiians would close ranks and refuse to let Lyons through in an effort to avoid violence in their temple area.

The moon suddenly emerged from behind a cloud. Able Team ran faster in order to intercept the six Russians from the truck.

The moonlight seemed to catch in Lyons's unkempt hair, transforming it into a halo of gold. His tanned skin seemed to shine because it was many shades lighter than the skin of the Hawaiians around him. In that sudden flood of moonlight, Carl Lyons's tall form stood out distinctly from the rest.

Taking advantage of the sudden mesmerizing effect that had come over the crowd, Princess Lilivokalani said in a clear voice. "Let Lono through."

"It is not Lono and this is not Lono's temple," the priest objected.

"We say who does what," Vorovski shouted, but he was ignored.

Mauna spoke, his voice betraying his nervousness. "The people called him Lono today. He both fought and finished the race. When he arrived, he saved the life of Princess Sherrie by deflecting a spear. At the Place of Refuge he saved me. What makes you sure he isn't Lono?"

"He speaks the truth," Sherrie added. "I do not see Kukailimoku, your war god, but if those men manage to escape with their prisoner, I promise you Kukailimoku will again leave his footprints on our island. Let Kukailimoku sleep and let Lono stand in for him. If you cannot accept this man as Lono, then let him stand in as Lono."

There was a muttering among the crowd as they absorbed the princess's logic.

"Shut up," Vorovski shouted. "I make the decisions here. Bullets put an end to superstition." He paused and forced a laugh. "You. You who wants to be god. Tell your men to drop their weapons and come back. Otherwise I will shoot these superstitious natives one at a time until you see reason."

**25**

Gadgets's concentration wasn't entirely focused on the enemy as he moved over the dark lava field to meet the Russian reinforcements coming from the truck. He knew he shouldn't split his concentration, but he couldn't wrench his mind from Lyons's predicament.

Lyons had completed a triathlon that had left many highly trained athletes in a state of collapse. Some were in hospital. The heat and the winds were the worst in the history of the race. Now he stood alone against six armed Russians. Ironman wouldn't start a shooting war because of the crowd of innocents present; the *spetsnaz* would feel no such inhibition. It was a no-win situation.

The full moon suddenly emerged from behind dark clouds and lit the lava field as if it were a stage. The approaching Russians spotted Able Team and dropped to the ground. The three Able Team warriors dropped to the ground before the Russians could fire. The game had become hide-and-seek on a sharp-stoned lava field. Whoever was tagged by a piece of lead would most definitely be out.

Gadgets, Lao Ti and Blancanales froze and waited. Experience had taught them to let the enemy make the first move to reveal both their position and plans.

They strained their ears, but all they could hear was the wind and voices coming from Puukohola Heiau. The sound of argument carried. The Russian's shouting carried. But none of the words reached them.

A scrape of rock against rock reached Gadgets's ears from the ten o'clock position. Pol was on his left. Gadgets signaled that he would investigate.

Gadgets moved in complete silence, a shadow among the sparse bushes and weeds. Concentrating on just one small area, he was able to avoid rustling plants or scraping rocks. His ability was so practiced that he moved rapidly despite his caution.

A plant whispered just ahead. The *spetsnaz*, feeling the pressure of Vorovski's summons, were trying to continue their forward progress. Gadgets froze.

A moment later Jaroslav Ocipovich's platinum hair flashed in the moonlight. He hadn't come prepared for a late-night game of tag. Gadgets buried his own uncamouflaged face in the dirt, wrapped his arms over his own whitened hair and waited, wondering if the movement had given him away to the hypertense Russian.

Ocipovich crawled within four feet of Gadgets. His technique was excellent by commando standards, but not as polished as Able Team's. Gadgets stayed frozen longer than necessary. He was considering his next move when another sound reached his ears. Again he hid his face and hair, depending only on his ears to warn him if the danger came too close.

Another Communist killer followed his leader's backtrack. It was an effective ploy in these circumstances and had failed only because Gadgets had paused to think through his next action.

Gadgets knew time was running out. If the other four *spetsnaz* had also doubled up, there was a good chance they would nab either Lao or Blancanales. Gadgets began his silent crawl after the second Russian.

The man paused when he came to loose rock, trying to decide whether to go around it or risk crawling over. Gadgets removed an anodized Gerber from his forearm sheath and moved into a low squat. Just as the *spetsnaz* decided to risk the loose rock, Gadgets sprang.

He landed on the Russian's back, causing the wind to escape from the man's lungs. Then Gadgets's left hand closed over the Russian's mouth and yanked the man's head up off the ground. The Able Team warrior's right hand drew the Gerber across the exposed neck, severing the arteries.

Gadgets held the head and mouth until the twitching under him subsided. He strained his eyes and ears for any indication that he had been heard and that another Russian would crawl over to investigate.

From his position, Blancanales also waited quietly, listening for the Russians' approach. They were good at their trade, but not good enough. There was the occasional rustle caused by their impatience. Blancanales repositioned himself and listened again. He wanted to be directly in the path of any approaching Russians.

When a *spetsnaz* crawled around a low fringe of weeds, he came face-to-face with the Stony Man warrior. Before he could react, Pol's left hand stabbed straight ahead, flattening like a spear blade. The Russian's larynx was exposed by his upraised head. Pol's hardened fingers crushed the voice box. The Soviet kidnapper coughed, choked and died almost instantly.

Lao Ti's *aikido* training had also conditioned her to let her prey make the first move before reacting. She crouched behind a rock to wait for the two Russian snakes crawling her way. She drew her MAC-11 from its leg clip, moving it so slowly that the first *spetsnaz* was passing her before she had the weapon ready.

Lao raised her leg and brought it down with the force of a pile driver. Her boot heel caught the crawling creature on the back of the neck, snapping it like a dry twig. He twitched once and lay still, unaware that he had been stomped into hell.

The second snake rolled to his feet, bringing his Small Frame to bear, but Lao's subgun, already filling her fist, spoke first. A three-round burst spotted his left cheek, the bridge of his nose and his right forehead. His brain closed down before making target acquisition.

As the Russian agent breathed his last, one of his comrades was zeroing his automatic in on Blancanales. In the bright moonlight, Gadgets watched the scenario unfold. Without a second thought, the Stony Man warrior launched himself at the *spetsnaz* killer.

A sudden burst of subgun fire from behind Gadgets made the gunman start and check his flank. The sight of Gadgets hurtling toward him caused him to forget his target in an effort to bring his weapon to bear on the new threat. The distraction was the only break the Stony Man warriors needed.

Gadgets knocked the gun hand to one side, brought his knees up and landed on the *spetsnaz*. Schwarz was moving too fast to maintain a hold. Momentum carried him over the Russian. He curled and rolled free.

The Soviet fighter rolled and tried to bring his gun into line again, but his time had run out. Blancanales's Beretta 93-R emerged from its belt holster under his shirt in one smooth motion. It coughed twice. The *spetsnaz* took both 9 mm arguments to heart. He collapsed back onto his face.

The three members of Able Team had accounted for five of the Russian kill specialists. They glanced around, trying to locate the sixth. When the shooting had started, the fair-haired leader had risen to his feet and had made for the greater safety of the crowd.

When they caught sight of Ocipovich, the Able Team warriors sprinted after him, not wanting to risk shooting into the crowd. The lava field was tricky by moonlight. Each patch of black shadow could mark either a slight indentation or a leg-mangling hole. The group was forced to hopscotch across the field.

The game required intense concentration. Every footfall had to be planned. The course through the dark shadows ahead had to be charted, and the enemy had to be watched. Ocipovich was the first to make a mistake. His head lifted momentarily as he checked the distance remaining. It was a lightning look, but Gadgets made use of it.

The Stony Man specialist stopped so that he wouldn't make the same mistake as the *spetsnaz*. As Ocipovich's attention returned to his feet, Gadgets spoke in a normal voice.

"Gotcha!"

The Russian was so startled by the quiet, confident tone that he looked back. He didn't have time to pick out his next steps. He stumbled and pitched headlong. Even as he fell, he tucked to roll out of danger.

But Gadgets had stopped and had his Ingram lined up on target. As soon as Ocipovich dropped low enough that he was no longer framed by the crowd, Gadgets squeezed the trigger of the MAC-10. The gun hammered four .45 slugs into the torso of the Russian before he hit the ground.

With the last reinforcement dispatched to Battalion Hell, Able Team jogged back to the ruined temple. No one voiced the choking feeling that they were too late.

CARL LYONS MOVED toward Friedrich Vorovski when the Russian threatened to start shooting Hawaiians unless Able Team dropped their weapons. The priest knew that there would be a confrontation on the sacred ground whatever he decided concerning the blue-eyed haole's embodiment of Lono. But at least the blond man offered a small measure of hope.

"We accept Lono's protection. We accept that Kukailimoku has sent his friend in our time of need," the priest announced. He was now firmly convinced he had made the only possible decision. He hoped it wouldn't cost too many lives.

Lyons's advance also forced Vorovski to reach a hasty decision. Vorovski's ultimatum had been ignored. Was this mad American so far gone that he could no longer assess reality? He really seemed to believe he was a god and, indeed, he was marching into battle with his bare hands against six automatics.

Vorovski moved toward the priest and thrust his Makarov under the man's chin. Immediately a new tension rippled through the worshippers. The priest was too concerned with his reputation to care about his life. He merely glared at the Russian. If the advancing American had noticed the action, he gave no sign. He continued to stride straight ahead as the worshippers parted to make an aisle for him.

The Politburo appointee realized his mistake the moment he pointed his gun at the priest. There were only six Russians and a huge crowd of Hawaiians. Shooting their leader could cause them to attack, and the outcome would be certain. The Russians could shoot some of them, but they would quickly be overtaken and beaten to death.

Only three Americans had gone after six *spetsnaz*. The commando conditions were exactly those for which the GRU operatives were trained. Vorovski convinced himself he had been foolish to try to protect the troops. He would simply kill this blond idiot. Ocipovich and his unit would take care of the other three. Then they could get to the coast and take their prisoner to the waiting ship. It was disguised as a fishing trawler and was in international waters. The Americans wouldn't dare to stop them.

By the time Vorovski had made new decisions, he was faced with new circumstances. The sound of machine-gun fire had told him that Ocipovich was not having an easy time of it. Vorovski swung his Makarov to take care of this so-called 'god' once and for all.

The priest and his fellow Hawaiians were still deeply offended that the Russians should tramp on their sacred ground. As Vorovski swung his automatic around to bear on

Lyons, the incensed priest kicked the Russian thug in the back of the knee. As Vorovski fell he fired his shot harmlessly into the air.

Two *spetsnaz* stepped forward and covered Lyons. They hadn't received orders to shoot, but that was what they would do if he didn't surrender. Lyons began to raise his hands. When they were a little higher than his head, he flapped them in the moonlight. The gunmen's eyes were drawn to the strange movement.

The first *spetsnaz* was still trying to figure out what the hands were doing when Lyons's foot introduced itself to the Russian's groin. The determined, ruggedly trained specialist managed to sqeeze off a shot before passing out. However, by the time his finger tightened on the trigger, the gun was aimed directly at the ground.

Lyons plunged his fluttering hands straight toward the face of the second gunman. The Russian instinctively moved his head to one side, giving Ironman time to bring his raised foot crashing down on the flustered killer's instep. The audience was so still that the sound of breaking bones carried to the fringes of the group.

Lyons's left hand darted down to catch the Makarov by the back of the barrel, stopping the hammer from striking the first round. His right hand followed through to the side of the Russian's averted head. Lyons's middle knuckle, extended beyond the rest, smashed the side of the skull, sending a deadly shock wave through the brain.

Cowley wasn't free to help, but he did what little he could. Two burly Russian athletes held his arms. The exhausted CIA man began to struggle and buck, leaving neither of his captors a free hand to use to shoot Lyons.

Lyons released his grip on the Makarov and grabbed the dead Russian's belt. He heaved and threw the body at the sixth *spetsnaz*, who was trying to get a clear shot at Lyons. The living *spetsnaz* cleverly sidestepped the flying body, but lined himself up for a jab from Lyons that smashed the ribs over his heart.

Vorovski rolled away from the priest into a prone firing position. He lined up his Makarov and held the trigger down.

Lyons stepped into the Russian goon that he had stunned with a punch to the heart. He seized him by the hair and crotch and threw him at Vorovski. The flying goon absorbed two 7.62 mm invitations to hell before falling on top of his killer.

Lyons leaped forward, smashing a spearlike hand into the clavicle of one of the two Russians holding Cowley. The thug collapsed as shock closed down his nervous system permanently.

Cowley found himself with a free hand. He swung it around and smashed his other captor in the face, then wrapped both hands around the Russian's Llama Small Frame.

The *spetsnaz* who had been kicked in the groin by Lyons had straightened out enough to draw a bead on the man who had given him such a generous helping of pain. Lyons lashed out with a lethal kick that caught the terrorist on the side of the head and rolled him onto his back. Then he leaped and came down on the Russian's chest, driving spikes of rib into his heart.

The body rolled under Ironman's feet, but he allowed the motion to carry him back to Cowley. He wrapped a long arm around Cowley's remaining captor while Cowley forced the Llama up and back. The pressure caused the Russian's finger to tighten on the trigger. The bullet entered his plexus and exited through his spine. Lyons dropped him and turned to Vorovski.

The small Russian plotter had extricated himself from under the larger body and come up on one knee. He held his Makarov at arm's length, lining up on Ironman's heart.

Ironman drew himself straight and grinned.

"You're dead," he told the Russian killer.

Vorovski thought Lyons's statement meant someone was covering him with a weapon. He jerked his arm around and tried to roll away from a possible line of fire.

Lyons took a long step forward, reached down and grabbed the small man by the neck. He heaved him clear of the ground and snapped him like a whip.

Dropping the lifeless Russian, Lyons turned to see the rest of Able Team. They were fighting to get through the spectators to help

Cowley and Lyons both paused to look at the dead Russians and the hushed spectators.

"This is going to mean World War III," Cowley breathed.

"Not necessarily," Lyons said.

He was still upright but had to fight to keep from swaying.

Cowley looked at him, too perplexed to voice his question.

"The CIA's covered all the deaths so far?"

E-4 nodded.

Lyons turned to the priest. "Mentioning this must be *kapu.*"

"It will spread through our own community. There is no stopping that. But our religion will have a better chance of reviving if haoles and the press do not hear of this. That much we can arrange."

Lyons nodded, and the priest hastened to spread the word to the worshippers Then Ironman turned back to face Cowley. Both men were now swaying from exhaustion.

"Have State tell the Russians that their entire crew, athletes, coaches, press, all the rest have been granted political asylum. Let the press have the same story. That'll account for their inability to find the Russians."

"I doubt if it will work," Cowley returned, "but it's worth a try. State will have no choice. They'll go along."

"Let's go," Lyons said. "I'm bushed."

Gadgets had just reached the cleared area where the action had taken place. He looked around at the broken Russian bodies that littered the sacred area.

"No blood has been spilled on holy ground, yet the desecrators have paid for their blasphemy," the priest announced pompously.

"You're bushed?" Gadgets asked when he reached Lyons. "You mean we're not going dancing?"

Ironman didn't seem to hear the wisecrack. Blancanales and Lao Ti supported him as he walked through a crowd. Sherrie and Ululani helped Cowley stagger after them.

The Hawaiians were chanting, "Lono, Lono, Lono."

## 26

Princess Lilivokalani's luau—finally held two days after the triathlon—was an overwhelming success.

The battle of Puukohola Heiau was the worst kept secret on the island. Journalists and tourists were the only ones who didn't hear about it. Everyone else felt compelled to come to the luau to meet the man who had stood in for the gods. The conversation was stimulating, the feast was more than filling and the object of their curiosity roamed among them.

Lyons wandered through the guests, smiling and nodding. He smiled only because it took less energy than snarling. He was too washed out to care. Finally, feet dragging, he found a chair on the lanai and collapsed into it, staring into space.

Nikko and Mauna approached Ironman's chair and stood indecisively. He said nothing, but stared at them with benign indifference.

"You saved my life," Mauna began.

He paused, but there was no sign of an answer.

The young Hawaiian took the amulet that was fashioned in the likeness of Lono from his chest and placed the thong holding the iron god around Lyons's neck.

"It's the thing I value most, next to the lives of my sister and myself. I want you to have it."

Ironman showed no sign of having heard.

Gadgets and Lao came up behind the Makananis and gently escorted them away.

"It was a beautiful gesture," Gadgets said. "When Ironman's not so far out of it, he'll be touched enough to growl at you."

Mauna smiled. He had been around Able Team long enough to know that the slightest acknowledgment from Lyons was praise indeed.

When Gadgets and Lao were again alone, but watching over Lyons, Gadgets asked, "Have you noticed that he's with us less each hour?"

She nodded.

Blancanales hadn't noticed. He had troubles of his own as he talked to Jane Briggs in a secluded corner of the grounds.

"You're doing what?"

"I've been trying to tell you for days, but you never had time to listen."

"I'm listening, now."

"I'm flying back to Washington tomorrow."

"But I just got off the phone to Brognola. We've been given a two-week holiday to help Lyons recuperate."

"But I start work Tuesday morning."

"Work?"

"Other people have lives and jobs, too. Hadn't you noticed?" Jane's voice was cold, determined.

"What about us?" Politician asked.

She bit her lip. Pol could see the sparkle of tears in the corners of her eyes. He longed to kiss them away.

"No. Danger follows you like a faithful dog. We tried a vacation, and you were nearly killed. I couldn't stand not knowing if you were going to come home to me alive when I kissed you goodbye each morning.

She turned and ran as the tears spilled down her face

Pol was about to go after her when Sherrie's hand closed about his arm.

"No," she told him. You've lost her. Don't make it worse on both of you. Let her go.''

Blancanales stood silent for many seconds before he could bring himself to accept the truth in the older woman's words.

"Come," she told him. "We must help Carl."

The Stony Man warrior followed her, wondering what she meant. For the first time he realized she wasn't alone. On her other side moved the tallest Hawaiian Pol had ever seen.

The man was nearly seven feet tall, but he probably weighed less than Pol. His wispy beard was pure white as was his hair. Both had been hacked off at shoulder height. The most unusual thing about the man was the way he moved with a slight sway to his body; it was as if he were a reed being blown in the wind. He moved silently with a grace that Blancanales had never witnessed before. Even Lao didn't move as smoothly.

The princess also rounded up Lao Ti and Gadgets. Lao had watched their approach. When they stopped, she bowed to the tall scarecrow. The Hawaiian answered with a slight bow, as a master might acknowledge a beginning student.

The five of them found Ironman on the lanai. The absence of Lyons's usual vitality was immediately apparent. It was as if the Able Team leader had died and a mortician had glued a smile on his corpse.

"Carl," the princess said.

He showed no signs of having heard.

The stranger reached out with a long hand that gently touched Lyons at several points on the head and neck.

"He has expended energy he never owned," the stranger said. His voice vibrated with power. "He must rejuvenate both his psychic and his physical powers."

Gadgets and Blancanales glanced at Lilivokalani.

"This is Kekupa'a. He is a master of several martial arts and our foremost authority on *lua*, the martial art of these islands. He has promised me he will do his best to see that Carl recovers."

"Come. A car waits for all of you. We have little time," the old man told them.

No one doubted him. Gadgets took one of Lyons's arms; Blancanales took the other. Lao Ti glided across the lanai and picked up the team's war bags. The tall Hawaiian led the way across the lawn to the car park. Able Team followed.

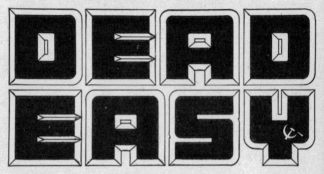

# TAKE 'EM NOW

## FOLDING SUNGLASSES FROM GOLD EAGLE

Mean up your act with these tough, street-smart shades. Practical, too, because they fold 3 times into a handy, zip-up polyurethane pouch that fits neatly into your pocket. Rugged metal frame. Scratch-resistant acrylic lenses. Best of all, they can be yours for only $6.99. **MAIL ORDER TODAY.**

Send your name, address, and zip code, along with a check or money order for just $6.99 + .75¢ for postage and handling (for a total of $7.74) payable to Gold Eagle Reader Service, a division of Worldwide Library. New York and Arizona residents please add applicable sales tax.

Remove from pouch...

unfold once...

unfold twice...

and they're ready to wear.

**Gold Eagle Reader Service**
901 Fuhrmann Blvd.
P.O. Box 1325
Buffalo, N.Y. 14240-1325

GES1-RRR

*Offer not available in Canada.*